CALLA ENHANCED

THE PIXIELAND DIARIES BOOK 2

CHRISTINA BAUER

Monster House Books
Newton, MA 02464
ISBN 9781946677792
First Edition

Elf portrait by Majorgaine

CONTENTS

ALSO BY CHRISTINA BAUER

APPENDIX

For All Those Who Kick Ass, Take Names
And Read Books

COLLECTED WORKS

Pixieland Diaries

Sassy pixie Calla loves elf prince Dare. Too bad he hasn't noticed her. Yet.

1. Pixieland Diaries
2. Calla
3. Dare
4. Winter Prince
5. Ley Queen

Angelbound Offspring

The next generation takes on Heaven, Hell, and everything in between

1. Maxon
2. Portia
3. Zinnia
4. Rhodes
5. Kaps
6. Mack
7. Huntress

Angelbound Origins

About a quasi (part demon and part human) girl who loves kicking butt in Purgatory's Arena

    1. Angelbound
    2. Scala
    3. Acca
    4. Thrax
    5. The Dark Lands
    6. The Brutal Time
    7. Armageddon
    8. Quasi Redux
    9. Aquila

Angelbound Lincoln

The Angelbound experience as told by Prince Lincoln

    1. Duty Bound
    2. Lincoln
    3. Trickster
    4. Baculum
    5. Angelfire

Fairy Tales of the Magicorum

Modern fairy tales with sass, action, and romance

    1. Wolves and Roses
    2. Moonlight and Midtown
    3. Shifters and Glyphs
    4. Slippers and Thieves
    5. Bandits and Ball Gowns
    6. Fairies and Frosting
    7. Evil Queens and Goblin Kings

Dimension Drift

Dystopian adventures with science, snark, and hot aliens

1. Scythe
2. Umbra
3. Alien Minds
4. ECHO Academy

This is a completed series.

Beholder

Where a medieval farm girl discovers necromancy and true love

1. Cursed
2. Concealed
3. Cherished
4. Crowned
5. Cradled

This is a completed series.

CALLA

DAY SEVENTY-ONE

ear Diary,
Today I dish out some ~~diabolic retaliation~~ harmless prankster fun on my new royal subjects, the summer elves.

Trust me, they totally have it coming.

Why the revenge? Yesterday, I held my first formal court as Queen of the Summer Realm. It should've been eight hours of chatting with my elf nobles.

Only no one showed up.

We are not amused.

Time to get tricksy.

This morning marks my second formal court… as well as some mega ~~payback~~ prank. While I write this, I sit upon a throne of red flowers. The shade goes perfectly with my pink hair, matching wings and violet eyes. Naturally, I have the pointy ears that mark me as an elf in terms of bloodline (although I'll always be a pixie at heart.) And let's not forget my ermine cloak; it adds a splash of white to the look. *Clutch.*

Yet appearances come second to my dazzling plan.

Although my subjects been avoiding me for weeks, that will end once the court doors reopen in just a few minutes.

I've so got this.

Sighing, I soak in the beauty of this moment. A huge atrium towers around me. Sunlight pours in through the open ceiling. The walls and tiles are painted gold. A pile of tiny purple bags sit in the middle of the floor.

Bonjour, le elf bait.

Those packets hold fairy dust, which is powerful magic that every fae wants. My prank is how these bags also contain… *wait for it*… a freezing spell. Grab one and you can't leave the room until I say so.

My scheme is so perfect, I can't stand it.

There will also be plenty of witnesses for my glorious success. My parents, Poppa and Muti, wait nearby. So does my best friend and major crush, Prince Dare of the Winter Elves. Let's not forget my buddy Bilge, the hobgoblin, and his piggy familiar, Oinky. Also, there are two summer elf guards —I call them Blond and Blonder—who hang out by the back wall.

Speaking of guards, they look expectantly in my direction. The time has come to set aside my journal—it magically shrinks into a locket that hangs about my neck—and get ready for the fun.

Prank on.

- Calla

DAY SEVENTY-ONE AND A HALF

~~D~~ear Diary,

When we last left my life, I was about to ~~launch my tricky revenge on the snotty elves who've been avoiding me~~ begin a lighthearted prank in order to chat with my stand-offish subjects.

My guards wait by the golden doors to my court chamber.

Heh heh heh.

"Let's begin," I command.

Moving in unison, the guards heave the doors wide open. "Hear ye! Hear ye! Queen Calla now holds her second formal court. All noble elves may enter and be heard."

I cup my hand by my mouth. "Guys, you're forgetting the best part." I gesture toward the mountain of tiny silk bags that sit in the center of the floor.

"Right," say the guards in unison. "Free bags of fairy dust!"

Staring at the opened doors, I brace myself for the onslaught. Any second now, a horde of elves will rush into this room, only to get caught like so many little spiders in my massive royal web.

Yet no one walks in.

I wait some more.

Still nothing.

Minutes go by.

Nada in the visitor category.

Hours slowly tick past.

And wouldn't you know it? Not one summer elf shows up.

In my fist, I hold the Scepter of Summer, a golden stick that packs all my queenly magic. I named it Sammy because that's how I roll. Now I lift the scepter, a movement that should inspire awe in my subjects and friends.

That doesn't exactly happen.

Instead of gasping in amazement, Blond and Blonder screech in terror as they race away. The main doors close behind them with a deafening slam. I'd be surprised, but my guards do this every time I crack out Sammy. Who cares that whenever I wield my scepter, I blow a few things up? Sammy and I will fall into a magical groove eventually. Maybe.

From here, things get worse.

My parents—along with Bilge and Oinky—rush to hide behind my throne. This isn't the first time they've done a *duck and cover* move from my spellwork, either. At least they're staying in the same room.

Dare saunters closer. Now I can enjoy one of my favorite views: the Prince of the Winter Elves. *Ah, Dare.* The prince is muscly and tall with strong bone structure and longish brown hair. Like always, he wears black body armor and a fur cloak.

"What magic are you planning?" asks Dare.

"Another summoning spell." I don't need to explain why I'm casting it, either. You can't rule subjects that you never meet.

Dare pulls his brows together. "You've tried that before."

"Only four hundred times. Something keeps blocking my powers. Maybe attempt number *four-oh-one* will be my lucky number."

"Just point Sammy upward."

"Good idea."

This room wasn't always an atrium; it used to have a ceiling. During my tenth attempt to summon my elves, I somehow blew off the roof. It's an improvement, in my opinion. More air flow.

In any case, my next summoning spell will be the ticket. I tighten my grip on Sammy.

"Here goes," I announce. My cheering section from behind the throne goes into action.

"We've always loved you," says Muti.

"Don't kill yourself," adds Poppa. "Or us."

"I brewed extra healing potion, just in case," offers Bilge. Oinky snuffles his agreement.

"Thanks, guys." *What else can I say? They mean well.*

I raise my arm high. Tendrils of golden light whirl about the top of the scepter. "I hereby command thee, Sammy the Scepter—"

Suddenly, Sammy melts into liquid gold on my palm. From there, he drips to the floor, only to reform as a sphere that's large as a human's basketball. And he proceeds to bounce around the room.

Not again.

Little click-clack noises sound as Oinky runs out from behind my throne to chase Sammy around the chamber.

I slump back onto my seat. Which isn't a good idea, considering how the thing's made from prickly roses. "I don't get it," I moan. "Sammy worked great the first day I wielded him. Remember how I blew up all the bad people at Lotti The Snotty Potty's Big Fat Fake Wedding? That was awesome."

"It was." *And Dare should know.* It was his body double that almost wed the Snotty Potty in question.

"And there's more," I go on. "I even rebuilt the Summer Palace after the wedding, easy peasy. But now Sammy's being a DISOBEDIENT LITTLE CREEP!"

I have to yell that last bit because Sammy and Oinky are now dancing around the far side of the room. For his part, Sammy pauses in mid-air, spins around, and then keeps right on bouncing.

Smart ass.

Blond and Blonder burst back into the chamber, see Sammy and Oinky, scream in terror, and then sprint in my direction. The guards slide across the floor on their knees, stopping just before my throne. I'd be shocked, but Blond and Blonder do stuff like this whenever Sammy's hopping around.

"A message, your Majesty." Blond holds up a large envelope.

"Thanks." I raise my hands. "Toss it here."

At this point, the guards are supposed to do some formal falderal where they step up to my throne, say a little speech, and then hand over any official message. *So annoying.* Earlier today, I issued the Royal Decree Of High Velocity Mail Delivery. Now they can just throw things at me.

Blond chucks the envelope at my face. Catching it, I tear open the message. *Boo.* A repeat. This exact same note has been sent to yours truly at least a dozen times.

Oh Queen Calla,

You are hereby invited to visit me at my palace in the Winter Realm.
I have information to assist with your reign.

- The Gargoyle King

I offer the letter to Dare, who scans the contents. "I can't believe he's still at it," says the prince.

Dare knows everyone in the Winter Realm. According to the the prince, gargoyles do indeed live in the Eidolon Mountains. They never had a king, though.

"With your permission," states Dare, "I'll take this back to my court. Perhaps my mages will find some way to detect the author."

"Sure. Have fun."

Dare slips the envelope into the folds of his cloak. The Mages of the Winter Court have been casting spells to detect the Gargoyle King's identity for days. Nothing has worked yet.

All of which is really beside the point. Writing in a diary means being totally honest.

So here goes.

Today's Fairy Dust Prank is a total failure.

My subjects are still avoiding me. As in, the palace halls are forever empty. People leave food at my door and run. It's unacceptable.

"Sammy!" I call. "Get back here! It's time to cast another summoning spell on my court."

My only reply is more boinging around the room.

I slump even lower in my seat, a movement which makes the rose prickles dig deeper into my butt cheeks. Maybe it's because Sammy always drains my energy, but I can't find it in me to care about a perforated butt right now.

Bilge tiptoes out from behind the throne. He's a squat green hobgoblin with a bald head, tiny eyes and pointy ears. Normally, tusks jut out from his lower lip. Not now, though. Bilge's big teeth just molted. As a result, my hobgoblin friend thinks he's a sexy creature. In fact, when Bilge talks these days, he sounds like a human DJ on a racy radio program. I constantly imagine saxophone solos playing behind him.

"I know why the summer elves avoid it," says Bilge.

"Let's hear it," I declare. "Can't wait."

Which is a total fib. We've had this *why does everyone avoid Calla* conversation multiple times today. I could live without another repeat. But this is my family and they're trying to help. And honestly? They might come up with something good.

"Perhaps the summer elves avoid *any* faeling," offers Bilge.

"That could explain things," I say.

See? Helpful.

For years, everyone thought I was a faeling, which is a human baby who soaks in enough magic to become a pixie or whatever. In Faerie, it's not exactly the height of cool.

Poppa and Muti fly out from behind my throne. They're tree sprites with crinkly faces, long gray hair and short white robes. Their little wings flap in a speedy rhythm. Is it weird to address ankle-high people as your parents? Nah. I got used to it ages ago.

"Bilge is wrong," says Muti.

I lean forward. "How so?"

"The problem are your pranks," adds Poppa. "You're not evil enough. Offering packets of faerie dust is just too nice."

This is an ongoing theme with my parents. *Calla is overly kind.* According to them, my soul will soon get chewed up by the other residents of Faerie.

"I'll work on being mean," I offer. My parents exhale with relief. I turn to Dare. "What do you think?"

Dare gives me the side-eye. So far, he's only participated once in the *why everyone avoids Calla* conversation. The prince's theory is simple: Sammy scares people. And the Dare doesn't have to repeat that concept; I already know what he's thinking.

I shoot him the side-eye right back. "You're wrong."

Dare winks. "I didn't say a word."

"The problem is *not* Sammy. My scepter is awesome."

"Yet when you use it, the scepter tires you."

"Only a little."

Actually, a lot. As a matter of fact, just lifting Sammy earlier today was a total energy suck. Not that I'll admit this to Dare.

"Here's what's important," I announce. "Someone's magically protecting my court from being summoned to my wonderful presence. Who? Why?"

Dare keeps working his side-eye. I can imagine his voice in my head. *There's one answer to all your questions: It's Sammy's fault.*

Sadly, in this case, Dare may be right. *Partially.*

"I suppose it could be Sammy... a little." An idea hits me. "I've got it! I'll practice wielding Sammy and show everyone what a great team we are."

Blond and Blonder race for the doors. "Run for your lives! The incompetent queen is about to kill us all!"

I really wish I could fire them, but they're the only two who enter my presence.

The guards aren't alone in getting spooked, either. Poppa and Muti flit away at double speed. "See you later, honey." They make a beeline out the missing ceiling.

"Oinky and I must also leave," announces Bilge. "It will draw my portrait while I'm gone." In this scenario, *it* means *me*. That's just how hobgoblins talk.

Bilge pulls a small vial from his pocket and drops it onto the floor. Matching puffs of red smoke appear around him and his pig. When the mist clears, the pair have also vanished. Bilge is a potions master, so the *puff and go* maneuver is his version of an emergency exit.

I roll my eyes. "There was no need for everyone to run. I didn't say I'd test my magic out *right now*."

"True." Dare tilts his head. "What was that about Bilge and a portrait?"

"Oh, Bilge wants to get a girlfriend before his tusks regrow. I said I'd draw him in his *less toothy state*. He needs it for some kind of dating exchange thing. I try not to ask too many questions."

"Indeed. When do you plan to practice your spell work?"

"First thing tomorrow. The Buttercup Forest."

"See you then."

Notice how Dare doesn't ask if he can join me? It's because I'd tell him *no*. He's a pushy prince when he's in the zone.

Dare removes a wand from under his fur cloak. It's a gift from my mother, the Ley Queen, and it helps the prince transport back and forth between the Summer and Winter Realms. He waves the wand. A cloud of blue magic surrounds the prince.

One second, there's Dare. The next, I'm alone. Unless you count Sammy, who still bounces up a storm.

Honestly, who could find him scary?

I decide to spend the evening in the royal library. Sure, I've checked the place a kabillion times, but there could be a book somewhere about wielding my scepter. Maybe it got stored on the wrong shelf.

And if that doesn't work? I'll try something else. I simply won't give up until I figure this thing out.

After all, that's what it means to be queen.

- Calla

Bilge

DAY SEVENTY-TWO

Dear Diary,
Today was my first official test with Sammy the Scepter. I might have melted the Buttercup Forest.
Oops.
- Calla

DAY SEVENTY-THREE

*D*ear Diary,
Second day of scepter testing. I got the Buttercup Forest back. All the trees can now talk. They keep saying how I suck at being queen.

Stupid trees.

- Calla

Dear Diary,

Day three of testing. Sammy was a total pain today. I spent all morning chasing his little bouncing butt all over the palace. Didn't cast one spell.

There must another way to find out what's wrong with my subjects.

And it needs to include a good prank.

- Calla

DAY SEVENTY-FIVE

*D*ear Diary,

Ba ba ba ba ba ba BAAAAA!

I now have a master plan for entrapping my elf nobles. Not to toot my own horn about this scheme, but *toot toot*. The brilliance of this setup is how it's based on the greatest secret in elfdom. In fact, if this truth were widely known, it could upend the very balance of power between Earth and Faerie.

I'll share it here anyway because although I'm now an elf queen, in my heart I'll always remain a nasty-ass pixie.

My Mind-Blowing Secret

Behold: If you wish to lure elves somewhere, just leave out a bowl of Cheetos. That stuff is elf crack. The end.

Amazing, am I right?

Last time I used bait, I chose fairy dust. Big miss. Someone cast a spell protecting my people from being magically summoned by yours truly. Since fairy dust is magic—or in the case of my scheme, magic that's boobytrapped with even more magic—it set off the protection spell. No one showed up.

This time, I'm using an elf lure that is magic-free. One might think the lowly Cheeto is not up to this mighty task. But then one would be sorely mistaken.

Mysteries of the Cheeto

One. You cannot enchant other foods into Cheetos. Magically-made snacks simply don't carry that special chemical tang that says *humans made this.*

Two. If you're a Cheetelf—*and yes, that's totally a thing*—then your treats only come from Earth. Which isn't an easy trip for most fae. For my part, I've been visiting the human world for ages. It's one benefit of having the Ley Queen as my secret mom. Long story.

Three. These days, my Cheeto collection is so large, I could trade it for a huge chunk of land in Upper Faerie.

Four. Yet I'm sacrificing part of my snacks in order to lure my new subjects, the summer elves, into a face-to-face chat. *Nyah.*

To set my trap, I choose the Sunflower Chamber of my new palace. It's a round space with a circular table in the center. As you may have guessed, everything here is painted in a retina-searing shade of yellow. After setting out a massive bowl in the table's center, I pour in five party-size bags of Cheetos.

Phase one of my plan is complete.

Waving my hand, I release enough fairy dust to create an enchanted puff of air. The breeze carries some chemical cheese odor out into the hallway and beyond.

Phase two, coming up.

Tiptoeing across the room, I scoot behind the door and wait. To kill time, I straighten the ermine cloak hanging over my shoulders. Underneath I still wear my favorite pink dress because COMFORT and POCKETS. In my right hand, I grip my scepter.

Suddenly, a stampede of silk-clad feet sounds down the outer hallway. *My prey arriveth.* Voices echo into the Sunflower Chamber.

"Stand aside!"

"You tripped me!"

"Allow me to pass. I rule the Blue Woods."

A herd of pale elves speed into the room. After a dozen folks surround the table, I slam the doors shut behind me.

"Ah HA!" I cry.

Shocked faces look up from the bowl. Somehow, in a matter of seconds, these elves managed to smear orange cheese fluff around their mouths. It's like I've joined a pointy-eared clown convention.

Scanning the room, I catalog the various faces. As I'd hoped, the most powerful elves were able to trip, elbow or out-magic their way in.

The group stares between me and the now-empty bowl. When it comes to Cheetos, these people are vicious.

"Have a seat," I offer.

No one moves.

So I raise my arm, showing off my golden staff. "Behold, Sammy the Magical Scepter!"

Silence.

"You really should clap or something," I warn. "He's kind of an attention hog."

Still no reply. Everyone stays frozen in their respective positions. It's like that human painting of the last supper, only with Cheetos.

Without any command from his queen, Sammy melts from my hand to reform as a golden ball.

"You asked for it." I roll my eyes. "Here we go."

Sure enough, Sammy—who now maintains his decidedly round shape—proceeds to bounce about the room.

I'll be honest. The first time my scepter changed into a ball, I freaked out and hid under my bed. But Sammy slowly rolled his circular self under the mattress and hung out with me for a while. I realized that shapeshifting is just what Sammy does.

And he's up to it again.

Boing, boing, boing... Sammy keeps bouncing around. Nothing gets knocked over, but it's certainly a great show. He won't stop until he tuckers out or gets some attention, so I let out an overly-loud cheer. Sammy then rolls across the floor and up my side. Once he reaches my hand, Sammy elongates back into his regular scepter form.

I try to cheer but let out a yawn instead. Something about Sammy doing his *bouncy thing* always makes me tired. What am I saying? Whenever Sammy does stuff, it wipes me out.

Meanwhile, everyone else in the room remains frozen in place. Before, I just thought they were standing around. Now I realize their eyes are wide with fear. Some even shake in terror.

This can't be right.

Before I came to the throne, Protector Lazare wielded Sammy for years. At some point, the scepter must have done its *spheroid thing* before the whole court. I shake Sammy.

"Come on, you must have watched Sammy do his *follow the bouncing ball routine* at least once."

There's no verbal reply, but quite a lot of shaking heads.

Never seen Sammy bounce. Now I know.

"Well," I state. "This is what Sammy does and there's no need to worry. Moving on." I plunk onto a chair. "Guys, please rest your butts." With robotic movements, everyone sits down. "So glad you all came here to greet me, your new queen. Let's start with the basics. Why have you been avoiding my royal self?"

Silence. Again.

I point Sammy at Lady Periwinkle. She's a tall elf who wears a dress made from indigo-colored leaves. Her long face and nose are accented by extra-wide eyes. A few wrinkle lines frame her mouth, which mean she's a very old elf indeed.

"Let's start with you, Lady Periwinkle. Okay if I call you Peri?"

"No."

"Too bad. I'm queen and you're Peri. Why have you been hiding from me? Your Blue Woods were lousy with blight. Seems logical to chat with *moi*, the person who ended that disease."

"You didn't request a formal audience," says Peri smoothly. The rest of the room seems ready to scream, pee their pants in terror, or both. Yet Peri is the picture of calm.

"False," I counter. "I sent you seven invitations."

At this point, it's important to note that elves won't lie, but they will twist around the truth. I call it elf double-speak. In this case, I did send Peri invitations, but they weren't formal decrees (not that she would have responded to those, either.)

Still, it's true that my messages were casual. Peri uses that fact for her double-speak.

"Seven invitations?" asks Peri.

"That's right. Not formal. But that wouldn't have made a difference, would it?"

"Oh, my," says Peri. *Which is yet another non-answer.* "Did you cast a spell to drag me into court?"

This is another classic move of elf double-speak: Answer a question with a question. I hate it with the fire of a thousand suns.

"I tried that and you know it. You've got some serious magic protecting you." I swing Sammy around once more, a motion that causes more gasps and general fear. "I cast summoning spells on all my nobles. My magic should have forced everyone to attend court, whether you wanted to or not. Some kind of protection spell allows you to hide from me."

"Seems like you found us anyway," says Peri. She licks from cheese fuzz from her fingers. *Sassy elf.*

"That I did," I declare. "I figured out that you're not magically *prevented* from coming into my presence. You just don't *want* to." I open my arms wide. "And now, we're all together. Two questions. One, who cast the protection spell? Two, why are you hiding from me?" I lower my voice to a conspiratorial tone. "Extra Yummy Bonus Cheetos if the reason you're hiding from me has nothing to do with Sammy."

What can I say? I like Sammy. This is not his fault.

No one answers.

I drag a big paper bag out from under my chair and plunk it onto the tabletop. "Snacks are in here."

Everyone leans forward in their chairs, pure hunger shining in their eyes. *They want these Cheetos, all right.*

I rattle the bag. "I'll start the discussion with question numero uno. Who cast the protection spell?"

A girl in the corner raises her hand. "It was the Gargoyle King." She wears a distinctive green shift of a chambermaid. I lift my brows, impressed. This chick shoved her way in here past a ton of nobles. And based on the major amounts of Cheeto dust on her face, she got in early.

"Gargoyle King, eh?" I ask. "He's a bit of a mystery. Who are you?"

"I'm Ivy, your Majesty." True to her name, the girl's dress and hair are woven through with living ivy. Butterflies also flitter about in her personal greenery. "I'm so honored for this chance to thank you directly."

After being ignored all day, I adore this attention. "Why is that?"

Ivy beams. "You freed me from the spell of being turned into a tree."

"Oh, that." At one time, I had a human friend named Griffin. Turns out, he was really Halcyon, an evil summer elf who'd been turning his enemies into topiaries. Looks like Ivy got on Halcyon's bad side. I must have freed Ivy through my many exploits during Lotti The Snotty Potty's Big Fat Disaster Wedding.

Ivy clasps her hands under her chin. "Thank you again. You saved me."

"Are there more elves like you?" *Because I could use some more support here.*

"That's complicated." Ivy eyes the bag hungrily.

"If you want more Cheetos, I still need answers. To recap, I first asked who cast the spell. Seems like the answer is the Gargoyle King. Moving on to number two. Why is everyone avoiding me?"

Ivy mumbles something that sound like, "mm-skr-mmmm."

"What?" I ask.

"Your scepter," whispers Ivy. "You don't know how to wield it. That means you're not ready to rule. That's why we all hide from you."

"Sha." I raise the scepter; everyone bolts under the table. Everyone except Lady Periwinkle, that is.

Peri licks at the corners of her mouth. "If you can wield it so easily, then show us."

Voices sound from under the table.

"Don't do it, Peri!"

"Hide down here!"

"Your life is precious."

"PUH-lease," I state. "You watched me kill Lazare with this thing. And Sammy just did his *follow the bouncing ball* routine not two minutes ago. What more do you want?" I thump on the tabletop with my palm. "Guys, get out from under there."

Which they do. It seems my people are easily led, if I can get in the same room with them. Nice to know.

Peri sighs. "I've been part of the royal court for seventy thousand years. No one has lasted longer. And in all that time, I've seen hundreds of monarchs kill themselves while trying to simply hold the Scepter of Summer. It's rare elf who survives."

"So I die from holding Sammy." *Peri is so full of it.*

"Exactly," confirms Peri. "The scepter will drain your

magic before sending all the power back into you at once. And then?" She pauses for dramatic effect. "You'll explode."

I can't believe what I'm hearing. "Explode."

"Ex." More dramatic pausing from Peri. "Plode."

"Like how I got Lazare to blow up?"

"*You* did nothing," snaps Peri. "That was the scepter. All summer elves know you're about to detonate."

"Come on. *All* summer elves?" I ask.

Peri sniffs. "The trees in the Buttercup Forest talk of nothing else."

"Oh, right. Them."

I take another facial inventory around the room. Everyone wears the same terrified stare. "You guys really think I'll get blown up by my own scepter?"

Nods all around.

Oh, this is too good. A this point, I should probably act all queenly and serious here, but I can't help it.

I laugh myself silly.

I'm taking head-back, deep chortle, and tears streaming down my cheeks. I might even let out a tiny fart by mistake. It's the whole deal.

"Look," I say after the post-guffaw hiccups stop. "I've been with Sammy less than a month, but I know one thing. He won't hurt me."

To accent this point, Sammy melts into a ball that rests on the palm of my hand. From there, he rolls up my arm and cuddles my cheek. I pat what I think is his back. It's hard to tell with a ball. "See? We're friends."

"And after your scepter changes shape, how do you feel?" asks Peri.

"Fine." *Lie.*

"What about your hair?" asks Peri.

"What about it?" I pull some strands around in my palm for a closer examination. Normally, my hair is bright pink. Now it's white. "Huh. That's new."

"We all saw it happen," says Peri. "The color faded as your little friend put on his show. I've witnessed this before. The scepter will drain you, little by little, before destroying you completely."

I stifle the urge to roll my eyes. This is probably a prank. Hair color spells are easy to cast. And sharing untruths that are designed to scare me? Just another trick.

"Do you have any proof of this?" I ask.

Peri taps her temple. "It's all in here. Check the library if you don't believe me."

"You bet I will."

"None of us wish to become collateral damage during your demise," adds Peri. "That's why we're avoiding you. We even toyed with starting a revolution. When your leader is a walking time bomb, then the people are better off having no ruler at all."

"Let me guess. That's where the Gargoyle King came into play." *Someone's been a busy little stone dude.*

Peri lifts her chin. "Yes, the Gargoyle King gave us a protection spell. That way, we can all hide from you until you're gone. And by *gone,* I mean, *dead.*"

I half-roll my eyes. This conversation isn't worth a full roll. "I got that part, thanks."

"The Gargoyle King wishes you to visit him in the Eidolon Mountains."

"I've heard. He's big into writing letters."

"And?"

"That range is lousy with ghosts. Even worse, it's surrounded by a null zone. I can't use my magic. Plus, it's too blustery to fly up for a visit. Which means you expect me to climb a mountain like a human? No, thanks."

"Still, I suggest you make the trip." Peri stares hungrily at the bag. "Now what about—"

"No Cheetos for you." I toss a party-size bag to Ivy, who tears into it with abandon. "Technically, Ivy answered both questions first."

While everyone obsessively watches Ivy eat, I lean back in my chair and think things through. This is a big moment here. In fact, it's important enough to break out a list.

What I've Learned

One. Some guy called the Gargoyle King cast a protection spell over my subjects.

Two. My people are hiding because they believe I'm about to blow up. Literally.

Three. Whoever this gargoyle guy is, he's trying to help. If he hadn't cast the spell, I might have a revolution on my hands.

Four. The idea that Sammy will make me explode is total stupid pants.

Five. I am not climbing a mountain human-style. That is yet another pair of stupid pants.

As I contemplate this news, Sammy rolls down my arm to take his scepter-shape in my fist. I stare at what should be a simple golden object. Could Peri be right? Am I a living time bomb? Or is this just an elaborate way of saying, *we want a different queen?*

Whatever's going on, one thing is for certain. This Cheeto break is way over. What started off as a trip to Prankster Fun Town is now rapidly veering into the Land of Dead. Plus I need to research both Sammy the Scepter and the Gargoyle King. That means a trip to library, not more hanging out in the Sunflower Chamber.

I gesture across the room one final time. "Good talk, folks. I'll leave now, being that I'm queen and have very important things to do." *There, that told them.* "Buh bye."

Everyone leaps onto my big paper bag in order to devour the remaining Cheetos. *Joke's on them.* Ivy downed the last bite.

All in all, my Cheeto Caper definitely worked. *Go me.* I shall now take a virtual victory lap.

In other words, I'm starting a new page.

- Calla

DAY SEVENTY-FIVE AND THREE-QUARTERS

*D*ear Diary,

Leaving the Sunflower Chamber behind, I march down the outer hallway. Ivy follows.

"Your Majesty."

I pause. "What's up?"

"It's late and your royal bedroom is that way." Ivy points in the opposite direction. "Would you like me to escort you? I was a chambermaid before Halcyon turned me into a tree."

"Thanks for the offer, but I know where my rooms are. Right now I'm headed for the library." Inspiration strikes. "Do you want to join me?"

Ivy pales. "But I'm only a chambermaid."

"And now you're my…" I twiddle my fingers in her direction. "My Leading Person for Personal Affairs." I wince. "I'll work on the title."

Ivy blushes. "Please don't take this the wrong way, but it's probably safest for me to keep my distance."

"Because I'm going to explode."

"Lady Periwinkle would know, honestly."

"Sure, she would." My tone drips with sarcasm, but that's lost on Ivy.

"Great! See you soon, your Majesty!" Ivy skip-walks away. She really is your classic happy-go-lucky summer elf.

With Ivy gone, I make a long and solo slog to the library. The place is another eye-straining experience, considering how everything here is coated with gold. I'm talking tables, chairs, stacks of shelves... even the rug gleams. Yet another opportunity to remodel. Eventually.

For now, it's best to hit the books.

I soon read through a pile of stuff. While I couldn't find anything on how to control the scepter, it turns out that there's plenty of stuff on how Sammy kills monarchs. The books were all hidden in a red box marked DEATH VOLUMES. No wonder I skipped it before. The titles are a lot of *blah blah blah you're going to die blah blah blah.* I'm not worried, though. Sammy and I have a special relationship.

There's also nothing about the Gargoyle King, but I do find more on the Eidolon Mountains. Nothing too shocking, however. The place is lousy with ghosts. From a distance, the mountain's snowy exterior looks like so many howling phantom faces.

Meh.

Far more worrying is how the place prevents you from casting spells. Also, it's blustery and cold, which is especially awful for summer elves. And, of course, the area is crammed with gargoyles.

Every time the Eidolon Mountains get mentioned on a page, Sammy starts bouncing again. I ignore him for a while. Until I can't.

"What is it?" I ask.

Sammy stops boinging around. For the first time, he takes a non-round shape.

The Eidolon Mountains.

From here, life gets strange. Semi-transparent blue cords curl up from the floor.

That's right.

Ghostly blue ropes.

Indigo in color.

And rising from the carpet.

My mouth falls open in shock. I stare at the twisting cords for a full minute. At last, I figure out what's going on.

These are ley lines.

My mother is the Ley Queen—she's also called the Blue Fairy—and she wields indigo-colored cords of magic. Ley power. It energizes both time and the connection between realms. You can't travel between Earth and Faerie without ley lines.

The sweet smell of lavender fills the air. That's never happened before. Also new is the fact that the ley lines are semi-transparent. After all, I've manipulated plenty of ley lines before, but those were always solid. These ones are ghostly pale.

What's happening, exactly?

Tendrils of blue smoke curl out from under the door and twist across the floor. The shade of blue is unmistakable. More ley magic. The clouds wind around me until I'm surrounded in a blue haze. Azure lightning bolts crackle around me.

I force my breathing to slow. This is strange, but it's not totally unexpected. After all, I'm the Ley Queen's only child. Her magic moves through me as well.

Little by little, the colored smoke vanishes. By the time it's completely gone, I find that I no longer stand inside my royal library. Instead, I now reside in a towering hall made entirely from white marble. One wall of the building has been blown out. A familiar figure stands in the opening.

It's me.

And I don't exactly look healthy. I'm all super-pale skin, sunken eyes and bony limbs.

My mother is the Ley Queen, which means she manipulates threads of time, including those of the future.

Is this a vision of what will happen to me?

And why does my life seem to suck?

Fresh blue smoke rolls toward me. Within moments, I'm surrounded once more in a colored haze. Lightning bolts spark nearby. When the smoke fades, I am once again back in the royal library.

So. That was weird.

For a time, I turn the experience over in my mind. On the List Of Recent And Strange Things, seeing the future is not a top item. I refuse to get cranked up about it.

Then it happens. A white line brightens across my palm. My heart lightens.

When that scar illuminates, it means that my best friend, Dare, is trying to contact me. Way back when I was fifteen—what would be a month ago—I had a vicious crush on Dare. It got so bad, in fact, that I'd always break out journal entries about him onto their own page. Now that I'm a mature sixteen years old, I have to stop giving the prince special treatment.

After this one last time, obviously.

- Calla

*D*ear Diary,

To be clear: I am not primping because Dare's about to visit me in the library. It's just that I have my routines. Before *anyone* visits my royalness, I always check my appearance.

Of course, there are exceptions.

I don't inspect how I look for my parents, Poppa and Muti. Or for my friend Bilge, the hobgoblin, and his piggy familiar, Oinky.

Other than that, no one really visits me.

All of which leads to a single realization.

I, Calla, Get Brutally Honest

The reality: My appearance-checking is really a Dare-only activity.

He's cute.

So sue me.

The end.

Whew. Glad I cleared that up.

Back to my *me.*

With Dare about to appear, I do *you know what.* In this case, I find myself looking classy in my ermine cloak and pink dress. In terms of pose, I lounge on a golden leather chair with a heavy book perched on my lap. Totally regal.

I whisper to the line in my palm. "You may visit."

A small sphere of pale light appears. The shape expands into what I call Ghost Dare. In reality, this is an astral body projection of the real Dare, but that's a mouthful.

I check out my new visitor because, hey, it's a good use of my time. Ghost Dare is crazy tall and broad shouldered. Longish dark hair highlights the sharp lines of his face. He still wears black armor and a fur-trimmed cloak. The guy must have closets stuffed with nothing but metal and furry things.

Ghost Dare bows. "Hello, your Majesty."

"Oh, drop it." I roll my eyes but secretly, I like the fact that someone else is acknowledging my new job.

Ghost Dare plunks down onto a chair across from mine. He eyes me carefully. "What happened to your hair?"

I hold up my book. "Don't you want to hear about my new book?"

"Calla."

Over the years, I've learned how to interpret the million different ways Dare says my name. Here's this one.

What Ghost Dare Meant In How He Just Said 'Calla'

One. He knows I'm holding out on him.

Two. There's no way he'll ever let it slide.

Three. But he'll humor me for a few minutes before he goes for the close.

With this in mind, I shut the book and rest it in my lap. "Did you see the title?"

"No, I was more focused on your lack of hair color."

"Want to guess what the title?"

"*Love at Court?*" Dare and I have an exclusive book club—meaning it's only the two of us—and we take turns selecting reads. One guess who picked *Love at Court.*

"Nope, this one's all queen stuff."

"Okay, I'll play along." The *for now* part is still out there, even if Ghost Dare doesn't say it out loud. "What are you researching?"

"Well, you know how my court has been avoiding me."

"I do."

"Well." With a flourish of movement, I set the book aside. This highlights how I'm about to share a great story. "Today I lured my nobles into a room and confronted them."

A smile quirks the corners of Ghost Dare's mouth. He loves it when I get all dramatic, even if he tries to play it cool. "And how did you manage that?"

I lift my chin. "Cheetos."

Ghost Dare gasps. "You sacrificed your collection? You've been working on that since age nine."

"Tell me about it. It's not easy being queen."

"Give me a moment here." Ghost Dare slowly shakes his head. "Wow. That's big. So what did you learn?"

I pull the book back up over my face. *Yes, I'm hiding again.* This part won't be easy.

"Stuff," I mumble.

"Calla."

"And things."

"CALLA."

It's time for another very important list on how Ghost Dare spoke this particular 'Calla.'

What My Name Means Now

One. Dare is worried.

Two. And frightened.

Three. Now he won't stop repeating my name until I share every last detail of what's going on, no matter how much I hide behind a book.

"Here's the situation," I state. "Someone cast a spell on my subjects to supposedly protect them from me."

"And who wielded this magic?"

"The Gargoyle King."

That guy's getting on my nerves," says Ghost Dare. "And before you ask, my mages haven't discovered anything about him yet."

"I did find some books on gargoyles in general. The best way to summon one is while standing outside at sunset. It's best if you can find a roof; they won't show up inside. Then you speak a certain incantation and—*whammo*—you've got yourself a gargoyle."

Ghost Dare tilts his head. "Which I assume you'll do soon."

"Tomorrow at sunset."

"Good." Ghost Dare leans forward and rests his elbows on his knees. "Why would this Gargoyle King cast spells that stop your summoning spells… and how does that relate to your white hair? Calla?"

See what I mean? The prince does not give up.

I squirm in my chair. "Well, it's a funny story, actually."

Ghost Dare isn't laughing.

"Turns out, the Scepter of Summer may have a not-so-good affect on new rulers." As if on cue, Sammy comes to life, collapses into a ball and starts vaulting around the room. I yawn. "Yes, Sammy. We're talking about you."

"The scepter drains you and that's dangerous." The way Ghost Dare speaks, there's no question in his tone.

I force my yawn to stop. "What made you say that?"

"Every time Sammy acts up, you grow weary. It's been concerning me, but I thought it was a coincidence." Ghost Dare's already intense gaze turns even stronger. "It will kill you, won't it?"

Sammy stops bouncing. Instead, my round friend rolls across the room to hide under my chair. "Now you've scared Sammy."

"I'm right, aren't I?"

"It's what someone told me today."

"Lady Periwinkle?"

I nod again.

"And the titles in Lazare's library? What do they report?"

"Some say that it might be lethal."

"Some? How many?"

"Fourteen."

Ghost Dare presses his palms against his eyes. "This is serious."

"No, it's not. Look at how cute Sammy is. He's a little bouncy ball of fun. Sure, he can be a tad draining, but isn't that the case with every friend who has some personality?"

"You need a plan, Calla."

"And I have one. I'll visit my parents."

Ghost Dare sighs. "You do that every week."

"But not with the goal of leaving Sammy with my D-A-D." King Tristan wielded the Scepter of Summer for thousands of years. If I leave Sammy with him for a few decades, what's big deal?

Dare grins. "That's rather brilliant."

"True, but there's more. I'll summon the Gargoyle King tomorrow. He knew enough to step in and cast a spell. Maybe he has some info on how to wield a *certain someone*."

Sure enough, Sammy rolls out from under the chair. Not sure how I know this, but I'm fairly certain he's staring at me in a way that says, *you won't desert me, will you, Calla?*

I give Sammy a wink. *He's so getting left with Daddy.* I'll leave some enchanted beach balls to keep him company or something.

Ghost Dare rubs his neck in a slow rhythm. "That makes sense. Would you like me to accompany you tomorrow?"

"The Gargoyle King is trying to help. Best if I meet him in a friendly way."

Ghost Dare frowns. "Hey, I'm friendly."

"You just growled out those three words."

Ghost Dare exhales slowly. "Okay, you're right. Best if you see him alone." He gives me the side eye. "And I'll be nearby."

"Thank you." *And I mean it.*

Ghost Dare's gaze turns almost worshipful. A new kind of energy fills the air.

I worry my thumbnail between my teeth and consider this turn of events. One minute ago, Dare and I were talking about my killer scepter. Now it seems like we're moving into more personal stuff. Am I okay with that?

No question. The answer here is a big *yes.*

Ghost Dare moves to kneel beside my chair. Things keep getting better and better.

"I can't stand the idea of you being hurt or drained," says Ghost Dare. "It highlights all the things I haven't said." He scooches closer. "It's like this. I've shared my feelings for you before."

Not this speech again.

"I remember. You said I'm like your little sister."

When Ghost Dare next speaks, his voice is all low and growly. "What if things have changed?"

Gulp. That's a shocker.

Reaching forward, Ghost Dare runs his fingertips along my cheek. Considering he's mostly transparent, it's a nice and tingly feeling.

"Talk to me, Calla. Would that be interesting?"

My mouth goes on autopilot. "Maybe."

Some small part of me screams that I'm insane. This is Dare, *my Dare*, the guy that I've obsessed over since I was a kid. What's this *maybe stuff?*

More of me thinks I'm making the right call. I'm a sixteen-year-old queen whose subjects think I'm ready to explode at any second. They're totally wrong, of course. Even so, this is not exactly what you call a stable situation. No way am I making any major plans or promises beyond *maybe.*

A long pause fills the air before Dare speaks again. "Maybe is good."

My eyes widen as a realization hits me. "You're scheming."

"Absolutely." Leaning forward, Ghost Dare presses his forehead against mine. It's both tingly and distracting. "Sleep well, Calla."

With that, Ghost Dare vanishes.

The moment I'm alone, my distraction burns into frustration. How can that be *all* Dare has to say? Our conversation loops through my mind on auto-repeat.

Dare says I'm more than a sister.

We shared some forehead knocking.

Then he vanished.

I also have the whole *exploding death* thing hanging out there, which—let's face it—is getting harder to deny with every passing second. Which makes it so much easier to focus on Dare. As a matter of fact, I've half a mind to go after him. Maybe if I magically pin the guy to a wall, I'll get some answers.

Only I know that won't work. I've tried it before, many times. Dare's tough. When he wants to keep a secret, the prince is a vault.

Not a perfect one, though. If I move onto topics other than Dare's scheming, then there's a far better chance he'll let a clue or two slip by mistake. Eventually. Right now, there's nothing to be done.

Back to my research.

There must be a book in here that proves Sammy isn't a threat. Or at least tells me how to wield him without exploding. As it is, there are far too many titles on Elder Elf Performance Issues.

Lazare was a weird guy.

I sift through another half-dozen books before shlepping off to my very large and pink bedroom. I did redecorate this chamber, by the way. Who'd want to sleep in Lazare's golden bed? The thought still gives me the chills.

When I do try to zonk out, I don't sleep well, no matter what Dare wished before. In fact, as I write these words it's now 2 AM. I'm way wired. Maybe if I draw a picture of Ivy, it will help me relax.

After all, there's a lot happening tomorrow. I've another attempt at holding court followed by a sundown chat with the Gargoyle King.

Fun times ahead.

- Calla

Ivy

*D*ear Diary,

It's my third time holding court as Queen Calla of the Summer Fae. Once again, I recline upon my throne of red flowers in a very big and roof-free chamber.

Although I've been sitting here for eight hours, not one summer elf visitor has walked through the doors. *Whatever.* I still have my parents, Dare, and the Bilge-Oinky complex to keep me company. Oh, and Blond and Blonder returned today as well.

All this lounging around is incredibly boring, which is why I've taken to writing in my journal.

Oinky snuffles noises nearby. Only Bilge understands this form of Oinky-talk. After a few minutes, my hobgoblin buddy turns to me. "Oinky wishes to play some more, but only if you approve."

For his part, Oinky hangs before my throne. At Bilge's words, the pig shoots me a questioning glance. It's his way of asking, *is this okay?*

"Have fun, my little friend."

In response, Oinky speeds across the super-slick floor while snort-laughing his little pink butt off. About half-way across the marble, Oinky drops onto his curvy belly and spins around pinwheel-style. His stubby legs jut out like points on a star.

"Be careful, Oinky!" cries Bilge. There's no real worry in his words, though.

Oinky hits the far wall. Afterward, he gets back up and runs in the opposite direction, his little piggy toes click-clacking on the floor before he drops onto his tummy... and the whole scene starts again.

Throughout all this, Sammy bounces around Oinky in festive arcs. The pig likes the Sammy's company, but Blond and Blonder aren't too thrilled. In fact, I'm pretty sure one of them peed their armor in terror.

Why does everyone fear Sammy?

Dare moves to stand beside my throne. "How much longer?"

No question what he means. Since there's no ceiling, it's obvious how the sun nears the horizon.

Sundown ahoy.

"Two minutes," I reply. "Then I need to see *you know who.*" I make claws with my hands instead of saying the name *Gargoyle King.* There are some things Poppa, Muti, Bilge and Oinky just don't need to know.

Muti's snoring stops. "It is over?"

"Oh, yeah," I reply. "You're done."

Poppa sits up and stretches. "What a lovely nap."

My parents then fly over to kiss the top of my head. It's a tree sprite thing. Afterward, they take off though the not-a-roof.

On the other side of my throne, Bilge frowns. "My Calla, I must take Oinky and go."

It's clear why Bilge wants to exit. Oinky's looking a little green. There's only so much spinning anyone can do before getting nauseous.

"Good idea," I tell Bilge. "See you later."

Blond and Blonder wave at me from their post by the door. "It is acceptable if we depart?" asks Blond. Or maybe it was Blonder. They're hard to tell apart.

"Sure, guys."

My guards take off. Let the record show that Blond leaves wet boot tracks behind him. *Ladies and gentlemen, the jury has returned a verdict on who was guilty of fright-pee.*

Poor Blond. Or Blonder.

As for Sammy, he returns to his regular scepter shape and leans against the side of my throne. This is his *sleeping pose.*

All of which leaves Dare and I alone. The prince sets his hands on either arm of my throne. He leans in until our faces are almost-not-quite touching.

"I'm visiting you tonight."

On reflex, I hold up my hand. "As Ghost Dare?"

He shakes his head. My stomach decides to compete in the Flip Flop Olympics.

"I'll meet you at your chambers right after your chat with the Gargoyle King."

"Oh, okay. See you."

I fly away so fast, there's only a contrail of fairy dust behind me. It isn't until later that I realize I didn't even ask what Dare was stopping by for.

- Calla

DAY SEVENTY-SIX AND A HALF

*D*ear Diary,
It's almost sunset.
Gargoyle time.

I hike up the swirly staircase to the Summer Palace roof. Sammy the Scepter stays firmly gripped in my right hand. With every step, more questions whirl through my mind.

Who is this gargoyle guy?

Why does he want to help me?

And most importantly, why would a random gargoyle know I need help at all?

The stairs end in a kind of wooden shed. Dying beams of sunlight peek through the gaps in the slats. My heart rate goes berserk.

Here we go.

My hand trembles as I push open the door. This tower's

roof is a square space that's about ten yards across. A waist-high stone wall encircles everything.

What's beyond the roof makes me shiver with awe. *Such a view.* It's one thing to walk through the Pink Forest, Golden Vale or Blue Woods—it's another thing to see these parts of Faerie from up high. My realm simply glimmers with light and beauty.

The sun sits about half-way past the horizon, so I figure it's time to cast my spell. I make three attempts while using the magic of my innate fairy dust.

No go. It's scepter time. Waving Sammy about, I speak the incantation I found last night.

> *Gargoyle, gargoyle, sitting still,*
> *On a rooftop perched to kill;*
> *What magic cast on growing night,*
> *Could lure you here to speak or fight?*

Since the spell isn't too specific, I add one more line.

> *I'm talking to you, Gargoyle King.*

Light flares from the scepter, casting a bright beam though the darkening sky. When the magic vanishes, my limbs feel drained. I let out the mother of all yawns.

There are four hefty posts on the roof, one at each corner of the square space. Now those blocks glimmer as if they're formed from black diamonds instead of dark stone.

And they change.

The posts stretch and grow, transforming into the shape of four massive gargoyles, one on each corner. Every creature has dinky wings, a broad chest, and talons on their hands and feet. Their flat heads are accented by a combination of pointy ears and wide mouths. The creatures lean back, spread their mini wings, and let out an ear-piercing howl.

My stomach sinks; I tighten my grip on Sammy. *Why did I think this was a good idea?*

Oh, yeah. Exploding death. Taking in a deep breath, I force my stance to straighten. I'm a real queen. Some random gargoyle dude can't frighten me. Much.

A small dark spot appears in the darkening sky. As the shape grows bigger, it's clear this is a massive creature.

The Gargoyle King.

Far below, none of my palace guards notice the newcomer. Normally, they'd try to shoot any intruder down with enchanted arrows. Not that their aim is great, but they'd have a ball trying.

Huh. Whatever magic protects the summer elves now shields the Gargoyle King from my guards as well. That's some impressive spell work, right there.

The Gargoyle King lands on a stretch of low wall before me. Meanwhile, the other four gargoyles let out another screech in his honor. The king towers twelve feet tall with a full head of dark, flowing hair and searing blue eyes. He seems to stare right through me, as if he can see every secret in my soul.

It's creepy as all get out.

The sounds of stones grinding fills the air as the gargoyle turns his head toward me. "I am the Gargoyle King." He has a super-deep voice. "The only of my kind of who fly."

Which explains the dinky wings on everyone else. *Good to know.*

"Greetings. I am Queen Calla and I summoned you here. Thank you for casting a protection spell on my elves. My people have been afraid of my new rule. Some even considered starting a revolution. Having your protection put them at ease. Your efforts are most appreciated."

More grinding noises as the Gargoyle King bows his head. "You are most welcome, Queen Calla."

I had eight hours to think through this next part. Over that time, I planned a verbal ballet of complex questions within questions. Now all those words evaporate from my brain as something blurts from my mouth. "How did you know about the Scepter of Summer?"

"Lazare blackmailed me," replies the Gargoyle King. "That evil protector heard about my skill with magic. After Lazare took hold of the scepter, he could not control it. So the false king stole away some of my gargoyles. Lazare would not return my people until I did something for him."

That story sounds like a lot of B-S. Lazare wasn't that strategic in his evil. Still, the Gargoyle King is helping me out, so I won't correct him. *Yet.*

"Wow. What did Lazare want you do?"

"Lazare wished me to cast a containment spell on scepter for him. I did so."

My eyes widen with surprise. "Containment? So Lazare never really wielded Sammy."

"Correct."

I bob my head and think this through. "That makes sense. Lazare was useless at ending the blight." For my part, I just grabbed the scepter and asked it to end the plague. Not too tough, if you actually wield the thing.

"Would you like me to cast a containment spell for you?" asks the Gargoyle King.

Since I grew up as a faeling, I've always been picked last in the Faerie equivalent of gym class. So I'm used magical folks giving me a hard time, not offering spells and assistance. The Gargoyle King's nice attitude seems awfully suspicious.

"Why do you care what happens to me? Don't tell me it's because you hate Lazare."

"I do not hate Lazare. I left my people vulnerable; Lazare did what he had to in order to solidify his rule. That's what it means to lead the elves."

"Not sure I agree with that whole *you have to get nasty to rule* thing, but go on. Why help me?"

"News of your great skills has travelled far across these lands." The Gargoyle King sighs wistfully. "There's your Macarena Caper. The Hairless Elf Council Adventure. Even your Bunnysaurus spell. You're the greatest prankster in all of Faerie."

Lately, I've been feeling like a wee bit of a loser regarding my future in general and as a magical queen in particular. But playing pranks? *Hello, happy place.*

My death grip on Sammy loosens a bit. "I'm glad you like my work."

"I cast that spell on your people for one reason—to protect *you*. With your permission, I shall now cast a containment spell on your scepter. After that, I can teach you how to wield it properly."

All of which seems to be something the Gargoyle King could actually do. Best to seriously consider this offer.

Door Number One:

Why I Should Accept Help From The Gargoyle King

One. Although I don't buy that Sammy will kill me, it's definitely annoying to get sleepy every time I have to wield my own scepter.

Two. This gargoyle guy is a big fan of yours truly. He's already been helping me out. What's so bad about relying on him for one more thing?

Three. Lady Periwinkle has faith in this dude. Sure, Peri's kind of a bitch, but that's makes her trust even more of an achievement. It's another check for the *Go Go Gargoyle King* column.

Door Number Two:
Why I Should Tell The Gargoyle King To Buzz Off

One. Everyone in Faerie is a lying liar except for Bilge, my parents, and Dare.

Two. That's it.

This one's a tough call. Behind door number one, there's hope for a future. Door number two means accepting a possible death by explosion. I look down to Sammy in my hands. "What do you think?"

Normally, the scepter would melt into a ball and do something. But it doesn't. *That's way odd.* Even stranger, I can sense magic rolling through the scepter itself. Sammy's trying to do something and can't.

I focus on the Gargoyle King. "Did you already cast a containment spell on Sammy?"

"Whatever do you mean?"

Now, I hate it when you ask for a *yes* or *no*, but the person answers you with another question. In my experience, that means said person is a manipulative skeezeball.

Door number two it is.

"Forget I asked," I state. "While I appreciate the offer, I'm not interested."

The Gargoyle King does a double take, a movement that involves more stone-grinding noises. "You're saying no?"

"Non. Nyet. Negatory. Am I making my point yet?"

"That can't be right." The Gargoyle King flutters his massive wings behind him. "You always say *yes*."

Now stuff is getting super strange. "What are you talking about?"

"You're a prankster. For years, you've been nothing but comic relief for the *real* rulers of the Summer and Winter realms. You carry a high pedigree, but what have your parents taught you that's useful in the slightest? Nothing. That's why you started keeping a journal in the first place, isn't it? You needed to change."

Ouch. Talk about getting verbally shredded. "After the battle with Lazare, I decided that I was a New-Old Me."

"Which is just another way of admitting that you'll be the prankster Calla forever."

"Hey, now. That's just cruel."

"Don't be surprised. This is what real rulers do. Or rather, it's what the ones who survive engage in. You've been fortunate so far, but how long do you think that can last? Even if you wield the scepter, the questioning of your rule will never end. And at some point, you will fall. We both know you don't have the strength to keep up the fight."

All those hours I spent practicing my speech for this moment, and now I have zero to say. Unbidden words don't even tumble from my mouth. It's all I can do to stare at the Gargoyle King as a little voice inside my head says one thing, over and over.

He's right.

The Gargoyle King steps closer and extends his hand. "Come away with me. I'll protect you. Rely on me to take every care off your shoulders. With me, everything becomes easy."

Suddenly, my mind echoes with every time someone called me a joke or weak. Why did I think I could rule the Summer Realm? My arm seems to rise on its own. It would be simple. I could set down all my burdens. Let this badass-looking gargoyle take it all over.

I reach forward. The Gargoyle King does the same. Our fingers get closer.

Closer.

My skin almost brushes his palms when it happens. The idea of turning over my rule makes me ill. My inner prankster whispers in my heart, saying that *we always figure things out in the end*. I lower my arm and change my mind.

"My answer stays the same," I declare. "No."

The Gargoyle King looms over me. "You have no idea what that choice truly means. I can hunt you down and hurt those you love. Is this really your decision?"

"Well, now that you're threatening me like a douche, it sure is." I raise Sammy. "Or you can hang out here until I figure out how to kill you. Your choice."

"This is wrong!"

Dark clouds roll across the sky. Winds blast in from

nowhere, whipping my hair and howling in my ears. The Gargoyle King rises to stand and fully spread his wings. All the while, bolts of lighting flare behind his massive form.

"You always say *yes!*" howls the Gargoyle King. "I'll never offer again. If you wish my help, you must come to me and beg." The Gargoyle King bares his teeth. "Your cruelty breaks my heart."

A classic circus tune goes through my mind, namely the one that goes *doot doot do de do do DOOT doot do do*. Someone's ready for the high wire.

"Yeah-kay."

The Gargoyle King takes to the skies and wings away. Once their ruler is gone, the other gargoyles hop off their perches and encircle me.

"Witness our power."

"Heed our king."

"Beg us to take you to the Eidolon Mountains."

"On your knees!"

My breath catches. These are four really big monsters. "No kneeling."

"Why not?" They all cry.

I say the first thing that comes to mind. "You're ugly and your mother dresses you funny."

Not my best insult, but does it ever get a reaction. The gargoyles stomp their feet, howl, and in general get pissy.

A low creak sounds behind me. The noise is barely audible over the storm and stone-grinding noises. From the corner of my eye, I find Ivy standing framed in the doorway.

"Oh my!" Ivy cries.

My heart lurches in my chest. *Not Ivy!* She wields barely

any magic. And here she is on the roof with a pack of gargoyles.

"Ivy, get—"

Before I can finish my statement, the four gargoyles stop. The monsters stare at Ivy in pure terror while crying at top volume.

"Ivy digs in her roots."

"The slow death!"

"She cuts!"

"Get to safety!"

The gargoyles quickly amble back to their spots atop each post. Within seconds, they've transformed back into what look like regular stone statues before melting into the rock once more.

The roof is quiet again. No storms. No gargoyles. Only me, Ivy and a lot of questions.

I crook my finger at her. "You can come out now."

Ivy takes hesitant steps closer. "The storm. Those monsters. There was no sign of them on the staircase."

"Yeah, that Gargoyle King packs some serious magic. My guards didn't notice anything either. And they love shooting enchanted arrows at anything that moves."

Ivy shuffles closer. "Royals must have strange things happen to them call the time." To Ivy, that seems to to explain everything that just happened. If she buys that line of logic. I certainly won't correct her. Ivy twists her hands at her waist-line. "I came here because I wanted to speak with you again."

"Go on."

"You saved my life and offered me a role in your court. I turned you down." The butterflies in Ivy's hair flutter extra fast, like they're nervous as well. "I was scared. But some things are more important than fear. I'm still able serve you. That is, if you'll have me."

My mind races through what just happened with Ivy and the gargoyles. It's common knowledge that you should keep real ivy away from stonework. Seems like supernatural gargoyles carry the same fear.

"That job is closed," I tell Ivy.

Her lower lip wobbles. "Oh."

"But there's a new role for you." I wave my scepter. A flare of golden light arcs through the air. The glittering power congeals into the form of a small golden butterfly. "Would you like to be my secret Butterfly Babe?"

Ivy's face brightens. "Do I get to keep that?" She gestures toward the golden insect.

This is a classic fae thing, by the way. It's like my Cheeto Caper. An elf will try to double-cross you seven ways in an hour. But if there's a pretty gift in the offering? All bets are off. They'll agree to anything.

"The butterfly is yours." I swipe Sammy through the air once more. The magical creature flits over to Ivy and lands on her fingertip.

"Oh, so lovely." Her eyes widen. "What am I supposed to do?"

"The butterfly will let you know."

Ivy bounces on the balls of her feet. "That sounds perfect." She skip-walks back into the staircase and takes off. Watching her leave, I shake my head. No doubt, Ivy wants to spend time with her new magical friend. It's what I'd do.

I spend a few minutes scoping out the roof and thinking through everything that happened. Questions zing through my mind.

How could I break a gargoyle's heart?

Why say that 'you always agree' stuff?

What does the Gargoyle King really want?

And did I make a huge mistake turning away his help?

The queries keep coming. There aren't any answers, though. In the end, I head back to my chambers. I want to draw an image of the Gargoyle King before I forget anything.

That said, I am *not* drawing the Gargoyle King's tail. I'll just pretend it's swaying at the perfect angle to be out of the image. Mostly because it's a long, rat-like number with an eyeball at the end.

Yes, an eyeball.

So. Gross.

Since I'll be seeing that in my nightmares from now on, there's no need to draw it here.

- Calla

Gargoyle King

DAY SEVENTY-SIX AND THREE-QUARTERS

*D*ear Diary,

Once I finish my drawing, a knock sounds on my bedroom door. Opening it, I find an empty hallway. A silver tray sits on the floor, compete with one of those domey-things that hide food.

When it comes to my life in the palace, this is pretty standard stuff. This building is filled with elves, fairies and *who knows what else*. Outside of a handful of folks—namely Ivy, Blond and Blonder—no one even shows their face without a major incentive.

And I'm not wasting any more Cheetos.

Oh well, there's nothing I can do about it now. And tomorrow, I'll visit my father. There's a chance Sammy won't want to hang out with Tristan, but that's not the only reason to stop by. Father's also a good listener. I've spent many hours sitting at his side and blabbing about whatever comes to mind. Sometimes it just helps to talk things through.

Picking up the tray, I head over to my mini-table for dinner. In this case, it's a bowl of galla root. *Yum!* I'm half-way through my meal when the door rattles with a distinctive knock.

More of a thud, really.

Which means it's Dare.

My heart beats at double speed as I recheck my outfit. I now wear a set of cute pink pajamas that someone stocked in my closet. Like my dinner tray, mystery folks fill my wardrobe with perfectly-fitted clothes. They even stuffed a drawer with my fave underwear—the kind that says *kiss my pixie butt* over the back.

Once I'm sure I look adorable, I head for the door. "Be right there!"

Gripping the handle, I pause before opening. Dare has been scheming. Is this the moment when I find out what it is? Can he be ready to declare his undying love?

Not that I care. I'm a queen now. Silly things like crushes on hot elf princes don't matter any more.

After yanking open the door, I find that one thing is clear. Dare has his worried face on.

No declarations of love, then.

Dare brushes past me into the room. "What happened with the Gargoyle King?"

I slide back onto my seat at my mini-table. "Mind if I eat?"

Dare takes the chair across from mine. "Calla." All he says is my name, but he's really sharing three things.

What Dare Really Means Here. Again.

One. He never cares if I eat in front of him.

Two. And he's been worrying about me.

Three. Details are a requirement.

So I launch right into it. "I summoned the Gargoyle King. He's a turd. More than that, he's a turd who's made of stone." I raise my pointer finger. "That sounded meaner in my head."

Dare reaches across the table and takes my hand in his. "Tell me what happened."

So I explain how the Gargoyle King showed up… then my refusal of help… next the kooky stuff about how I supposedly break the king's heart… the way the other gargoyles tried to scare me… and finally, how Ivy unwittingly saved the day. In between, I cover in detail how the Gargoyle King said I was too nice to rule and needed his help.

Dare gives my hand a gentle squeeze. "You did really well, Calla. He was trying to bully you and you held your ground. That's my Old-New Calla."

"You're my friend. You're supposed to say I'm awesome."

"Maybe I'll show you with actions instead of words."

I bob my brows. "You're scheming again."

"Absolutely." Dare leans across the table, stopping when our mouths are inches apart. "And you're not getting anything else out of me today."

I stick out my tongue at him. Talking to Dare always makes me feel better. Not sure why it works, I'm just glad it does.

"Then tell me about gargoyles in general," I state. "They do live in your realm after all."

"I can share one thing," says Dare. "Those gargoyles last night must have been terrified. We don't have much in the way of green things in the Winter Realm. It's true that ivy plants eventually tear apart real stone, but that process takes years. Don't bother explaining that to gargoyles, though. They think they'll be destroyed in seconds."

"I gave Ivy an enchanted butterfly so I can summon her again, just in case. She's now my official Butterfly Babe."

"Clever. Will you reach out to the Gargoyle King again?"

"Nah." I finish my last bite, lean back in my chair and pat my belly. *Nothing's better than galla root.* "Next on my list is visiting Father. No court tomorrow. Instead, I'll hit Earth."

"In that case, I'll go with you," declares Dare.

"I appreciate it, but—"

"Not a chance." Dare leans forward. "I'm playing my *over-protective friend card* here. It's one thing when I can lurk nearby in case of trouble. But if you're in a completely different realm, that's unacceptable."

I narrow my eyes. "Friend card."

Dare's gaze does that *intense thing* again. "For now."

I've known Dare since forever. In this moment, he's thinking about what we discussed last night.

And I'm thinking about it, too.

At this point, I should play it cool. If Dare knows I'm still interested in his mystery *more than friends* scheme from yesterday, then he'll never say a word.

So of all the things I should do right now, pressing Dare for more info is last on the list.

Which is why I sit here.

Quietly.

This is me, not saying a word.

I tap my spoon against my bowl.

Tap.

Tap.

Tap.

Gah.

"How is your secret scheme going?" I ask.

Shockingly enough, Dare actually answers.

"Slowly. There are some obstacles."

I know this guy. For Dare, replying with *slowly* and *there are some obstacles* is a massive amount of information. I could do a victory lap around my own bedchamber.

"I have other news," continues Dare. "I did uncover some information on the Gargoyle King. He has a castle at the top of Eidolon Mountain called Alabaster Hall." The lines of Dare's face pull tight with grief. "You know what's also on that mountain."

"The Winter Citadel… and Reiver's grave."

"That's right."

Reiver was Dare's older brother. It was Reiver, Halcyon and Lazare who tried to assassinate my father. To survive the attack, Tristan put himself into an enchanted sleep.

Dare sighs. "I never told you about Reiver's death."

"You don't have to say anything."

"We live in a magical realm. There are no coincidences. The Gargoyle King has a secret castle near the very spot where *your* father was attacked by *my* brother. You need to know the full truth."

"Good point."

I can't help but notice how the muscles twitch in Dare's neck. The guy is really upset.

"After the attack, Mother and I found Reiver's body in the Winter Citadel." Dare swallows. "His throat was cut. The blade's edge was distinctive. At the time, I thought it was Tristan's weapon. I figured your father fought back against Reiver." Dare's voice breaks. "But I saw that distinctive edge again one month ago, when I was fighting Halcyon in the royal duel."

Which Dare totally won, but the way.

I gasp. "Do you think Halcyon killed Reiver?"

Dare nods. "Halcyon, Reiver, and Lazare were all working together to assassinate your father. For some reason, things went wrong. Halcyon must have killed my brother."

My next question is a rough one. I'm asking about Dare's mother, after all.

"What about Saita? Do you think your mother was involved in the assassination?"

Dare exhales slowly. "The winter court prides itself on treachery. Anything is possible."

My heart sinks. Dare's Winter Realm is not so much a *world of snow* as a *den of vipers*.

"There's more," adds Dare. "I've always suspected Saita and Lazare had some kind of relationship."

A memory appears: Saita playing footsie with Lazare at Lotti's fake wedding. I've no plans to share details with Dare —some stuff you don't need to know about your mother—but I can confirm his point in a general way.

"A relationship," I echo. "Seems legit."

"We should bring up the assassination attempt as well as the Gargoyle King at the next Elven Council."

My mouth twists with disgust. "Ugh. Is that tomorrow?"

"It is."

I slump even lower in my chair. It's official. This is a lot for me to process. Becoming queen. Having no-show subjects. Sammy possibly killing me. And the Gargoyle King being a creepster fanboy.

Bleugh.

I throw up my hands. "I've had it with this whole scene."

Dare's seen me like this before. We call it my Pixie Meltdown Mode.

The prince goes right into action.

After whipping off his cloak, Dare crosses the room, kicks off his boots, and then sits with his back against the headboard of my bed. And just because Dare is that kind of guy, his socks come off with his boots. His bare feet peep out from under his leather pants.

I'm a sucker for cute guy feet.

With a practiced movement, Dare unlatches his leather upper body armor and tosses it aside, revealing the Henley-style shirt he wears underneath. I rarely get to experience Dare without his cloak, let alone without his upper body armor.

The prince pats the mattress beside him. "Over here," he orders.

He doesn't need to ask me twice. After crossing the room, I curl up beside Dare on the mattress. My head rests against his shoulder. For a big dude, Dare is a very cuddly guy. Things get even better when the prince starts twiddling my hair.

We don't say a word. It's just good to be together with less body armor in the equation.

I fall asleep like it's my job.

- Calla

*D*ear Diary,

When I wake up, Dare is gone but I've been carefully tucked under the comforter. I smile my face off.

Then I remember.

Today I'm supposed to join the Elven High Council. This is a disaster of a major variety. Here's why.

What Sucks About The Elven High Council

One. Before I became queen, the council was super nasty to me. Namely, they kept complaining about my pranks.

Two. They had no right to whine since I pulled some pretty amazing tricks. The finest is the Lazare Poop Parade, an achievement which involved goblets of enchanted wine and a long line for the bathroom.

Three. The council was directly involved with my being locked up in a supernatural prison. I escaped, but it's the point that counts.

Long story short, visiting the Elven High Council isn't exactly top of my *to do list*.

Even so, I'm queen now and that means doing a lot of stuff that isn't too much fun. Hopefully, the visit won't take long. I still plan to visit Earth today and see Father.

And hopefully stop myself from dying.

The denial phase of the whole Sammy situation is getting harder by the minute.

Once I'm ready, I head off to the Pinnacle, which is a pokey dark castle with a lot of gloomy big chambers. It's also where the council always gets together. Once inside, I fly into the meeting room, plunk onto my golden throne, and wait.

And wait.

More waiting.

Finally, some folks step into the chamber. It's Saita, the Queen of the Winter Realm, and Dare.

And that's everyone. *Huh.*

Saita slides onto the throne next to mine. She's tall and pale with long black hair. Her white gown glitters like fresh snow on a winter morning. While my seat is all golden, her throne is pointy, dark, and made from black granite. Dare moves to stand beside her.

"Where is everybody?" I ask.

"It's just us today," explains Saita.

"This was not discussed beforehand," snaps Dare. "We wasted valuable time sending the other council members away."

Saita focuses on her son. "You know the rules. Do not speak unless I address you or I shall enforce your silence with magic."

Which she most definitely can do. Not much tops regal magic.

I scrunch up my face and consider things. Saita sent everyone away? It's not like these councils are packed as it is. Maybe a dozen nobles show up, and I'm including both the Summer and Winter Realms. And with my elves avoiding me, the audience promised to be even smaller.

What does Saita plan that she can't even have her own people witness?

Good question, me.

It's no secret that Saita is a wild card. Sometimes, she does amazingly helpful things. For instance, Saita once slipped my dungeon guards some enchanted wine so Dare and I could escape. In other instances, she's just a card carrying meanie.

Saita rounds on me. "Do you have anything you'd like to discuss?"

I've had plenty of time to think this over, so I launch right into my reply. "I wish to open investigations into the Gargoyle King, my father's attempted assassination, and Reiver's death."

A look of genuine terror flashes across Saita's face. The expression is gone too quickly to be certain, though. "Interesting ideas. First, we must discuss a more pressing topic. I assume your successor is Lazare's eldest surviving daughter. Can you confirm this?"

I scrunch up my features in confusion. "Are you serious? I've never met any daughter but Lotti."

"So you'd see no reason to break a familial line of succession. Perfect." Saita unfurls her elfy wings and flies from the room at top speed.

Wish I could pretend she's doing something to help, but I have a sinking suspicion Saita is in meanie mode.

"What was that?" I ask Dare.

"I've no idea. But I don't like it."

The hairs on the back of my neck stand on end. There's no avoiding that only Dare and I are the only ones left in the room. Meanwhile, Saita is hatching some evil plans. *She wouldn't go after Dare, would she?*

"Mind if I ask you something personal?"

"Never."

"If you mother wanted to hurt you, could she?"

"Not directly. Ancient magic that prevents royals of the same realm from killing each other."

"So they use someone else for their dirty work."

"Precisely."

My thoughts turn back to the assassination attempt on Father. If Lazare and Halcyon wanted to kill their king, magic would stop them from doing it directly, since all three are Summer nobles. The magic wouldn't have prevented Reiver from playing assassin, though.

If Saita wanted to off Dare, what third party would she send?

Across the room, the main doors slam shut. The walls melt from dark granite to a distinctive mixture of stone and diamonds.

I've seen this before.

Namely, last night at sunset.

Faces appear in the walls. *Gargoyles.* Seconds later, no less than twenty massive creatures leap from the great stone panels towering around us. This particular chamber is massive, but with so many monsters around us, the place suddenly feels small.

New question: *Does Saita wish to kill both me and her son?*

The gargoyles get rowdy.

"Calla! Calla! We kill Calla!"

"Run away puny prince!"

"Beg for mercy, little queen, and we no kill!"

I roll my eyes. Here I am, worrying about Saita wanting to destroy her son. All the while, the Winter Queen (or someone else just as nasty) just wants to kill me.

I focus on Dare. "Don't take this the wrong way, but your mother can be an icy bitch."

"Wait until you meet more of my winter court."

If I ever meet them, says a tiny voice in the back of my head.

"Oh well," I sigh. "These gargoyles aren't going to destroy themselves." I look to Dare. "What takes these guys down? The books I found were a little vague."

Dare raises his hands. Spheres of pale power appear above his palms. "This is what you call a *great learning opportunity*."

"So we've no idea how to destroy them."

"Correct. I vote for a volley of destructive magic."

"Works for me."

I slide off the throne and wave Sammy around. An arc of golden light follows the movement. The magical brightness congeals into a small butterfly that hovers a few inches before my face.

"Get Ivy," I order the butterfly. The little creature zooms off in an arc of light.

"Good idea," states Dare.

The gargoyles stalk in closer.

"Plead to see our King!"

"Grovel!"

"Run for safety, elf man."

"Beg us to take you to the Eidolon Mountains, little queen."

With that, the great *is Saita behind this* debate is officially over. This attack is one hundred percent the work of the Gargoyle King.

Dare lifts his arms. Spheres of power appears on his palms, casting beams of light across the room. "I am Prince Dare of the Winter Realm. If you value your existence, you will come no closer."

"We've no problem with you."

"This one belongs to our king."

Dare's face goes angry as thunder. "Belongs to who?"

"Spot on, Dare." I hold Sammy high. "I belong to *me.*"

Dare and I share a look. This isn't our first time going into battle together. Sure, gargoyles are different than fighting geriatric unicorns or miniature trolls. Still, in every fight there's a moment where Dare and I exchange an enraged look. Then we go on fighting.

That's what happens now. Moving together, the prince and I break our stare. Next I send out bolt after bolt from Sammy. All the while, I picture the magic exploding one gargoyle after another, just like I did to Lazare. It's the only spell I know, and I'm leaning into it. I also throw in some better insults, because that's just fun. My favorite is calling them block heads. It's both a pun and easy to remember.

At the same time, Dare shoots off multiple orbs of power that slam into different gargoyles. Smoke fills the air. An ethereal wind whips through the chamber. Howls sound. Chunks of floor and wall go flying.

This goes on for a while until things turn oddly quiet. Dare and I stop casting. Dust particles slowly settle to the floor. Seconds pass while we wait for the chamber to become visible again. My pulse beats so hard, I feel it in my throat. I scan the room, wondering how many gargoyles were left.

The answer?

All of them.

A foul taste creeps into my mouth. *Oh, no.*

Dare and I sent our best spells at these creatures and nothing made a dent. The same can't be said for the gargoyles, though. They went to town on the chamber. All the floor tiles are uneven or smashed to bits. Huge chunks are missing from the walls. The ceiling now lurches at an odd angle.

This isn't good.

Dare and I share another glance. This one isn't filled with rage. Instead, we're both consumed by shock. Not one chip is gone from these creatures. *What the WHAT?* A shiver runs up my spine.

Beyond magically exploding these gargoyles, I got nothing.

Suddenly, the main door whips open. Ivy flies through while riding a massive golden butterfly. I grin. That little insect expands into butterfly horse for transit.

Nice work, self and Sammy.

Ivy pumps her fist in the air. "Butterfly Babe to the rescue!"

The gargoyles lose their minds.

"Ivy tears."

"She kills!"

"Get to safety!"

The gargoyles rush back to he walls, where they merge once again into the stone. Within seconds, they've all vanished.

Ivy dismounts her butterfly and beams. "That was great!"

Dare bows. "We are in your debt, oh Butterfly Babe."

She blushes something fierce. "You're welcome, Sir Winter." That's not his title, but there's no way I'm correcting Ivy right now. She turns to me. "I love my new job."

I shoot her a thumbs up. "You're the best... You're my

only…" I try to finish my thought, but the words seems stuck in the back of my mind.

All of a sudden, my legs feel wobbly beneath me.

Dare stalks closer. "You cast too many spells with the scepter. It's time to rest."

I open my mouth, ready to argue the point, then drop it. "You're right. I am sleepy sleeper sleep."

Not my best reply.

My legs give out just as Dare scoops me into his arms. I'd say that I enjoyed the cuddle, but I was too exhausted to really appreciate anything.

At some point, Dare unfurls his wings. I'm sad to miss this as well. The prince's wings are cool, what with their dark feathers and raven-style action. In stead of appreciating the view, I nod off in transit.

At some point, I realize that I've returned to my chambers. Someone magically changed me into pajamas and tucked me into bed. I don't remember much about the whole experience beyond Dare being around. Somehow, I manage to get out a few words.

"Father… tomorrow."

Dare says that's fine, considering how he's still going with me.

Once the prince is gone, I force myself to write this journal entry because you never know what will be important later. And these gargoyles are tricky in terms of how they melt out of the walls—I'll be sure to sketch that while it's fresh, too.

But once that's done, I am so conking out. Maybe for a year.

- Calla

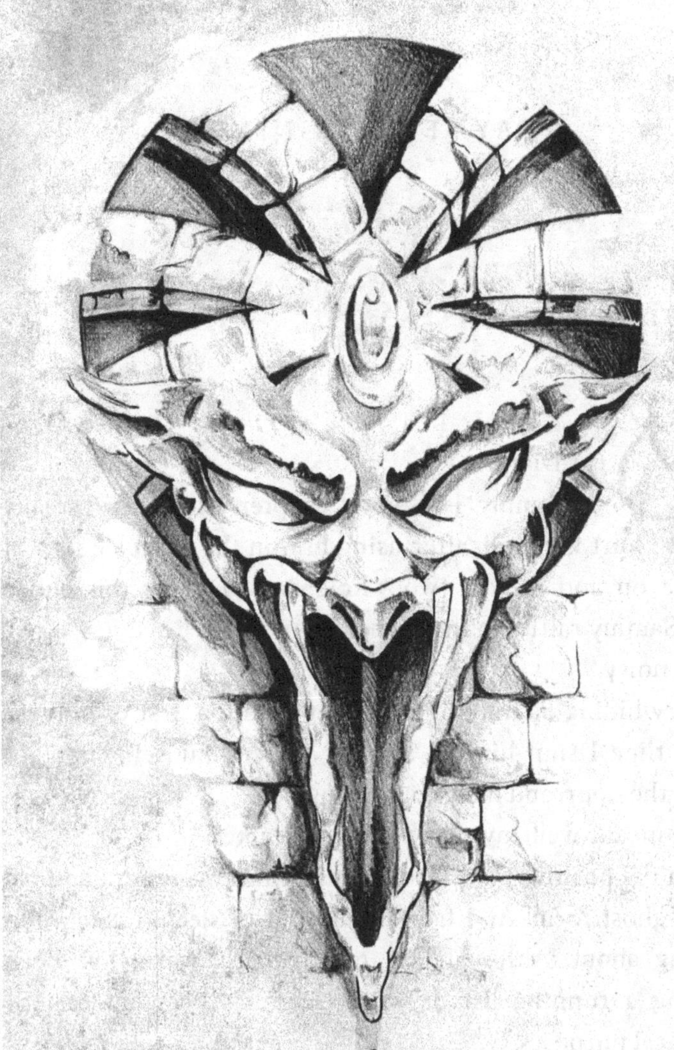

Gargoyles Appear

*D*ear Diary,

Sammy is a good scepter. He doesn't really want to hurt me. Still, after using him in the gargoyle fight, I snooze on and off for two whole days. During this entire time, Sammy rattles in the corner.

So noisy.

I try hiding Sammy in the closet within a nest of pillows. Every time I shut him in, Sammy flattens himself, slips out under the door, and hangs out by my bed.

He means well, my shape-shifting scepter.

On the positive side, Dare keeps coming around… and *not* in his ghost form. As I fade in and out of sleep, I catch him moving about. Although I'm mostly half awake, I've been keeping a running list of what Dare has been up to. For historical purposes.

Cute Stuff That Dare Does

One. Feeds me mushed-up galla root.

Two. Gets me to drink healing potions from Bilge.

Three. Brings in Poppa and Muti to visit. They even get a mini pillow to sleep by my head.

Four. Reads something called *Grimm's Fairy Tales* to me. What a hoot.

Five. Sleeps in a hefty chair by my bed at night.

Six. Wears a dark Henley-style top and leather pants without socks *all the time*. I'm thinking about casting a hiding spell on his body armor.

Ivy offers to help out, but Dare shoos her off. I'm glad. The rest of my subjects are still avoiding me, so it all works out.

Kind of.

There is one problem. Every so often, I catch Dare staring at me. It's not his yummy look—and by that I mean the one that gets me all squishy inside—but something else.

Finally, I can't take it anymore. I set my journal aside, sit up and round on Dare.

"You're doing that thing," I state.

"What thing?"

"Over worrying."

Dare nods. "That scepter is bad news."

Sammy knows we're talking about him, so he starts rattling on the floor.

"We know you don't mean it," I tell Sammy. "Besides, I have a plan."

Dare leans forward. "Which is?"

"See Tristan."

"True."

"And we'll visit today."

"Better to rest now." Dare tucks the comforter under my chin. "We'll go tomorrow together."

"But I have to—"

"Write in your journal first, I know. I won't peek."

And he doesn't.

- Calla

*D*ear Diary,

Today I visit my father.

As I get ready for my trip, nervous energy careens through me. I even have trouble zipping myself into my pink battle leathers. If Father can babysit Sammy, it will solve all my death issues, fast.

Dare arrives—in body armor and furs, naturally—and together we head to the Buttercup Forest. For me to travel to Earth, I must pull up some ley lines from the ground. The forest is a choice spot.

Or it used to be.

Now that the trees can talk, it gets a little dicey.

Once we reach the forest, I kneel beside a particularly sunny looking group of trees. After reaching into the ground, I search for the ley lines that connect the realm of Faerie with Earth. The trees decide to offer some commentary. Fortunately, they're in a good mood today.

"And Queen Calla goes for the ley line."

"She has the look of a champion, ladies and gentlemen."

"She. Could. Go. All. The. Way."

And when I finally grab a blue ley line and pull it from the ground?

"Get out the baskets boys, it's harvest time!"

With the glowing blue cord in my hands, I then twist it into a door shape. The bright line quickly solidifies into what looks like a blue wooden door. I pull on the handle here in Faerie and the door opens to the familiar hillside outside Glover's Hollow, NY.

And I did all this without needing to use Sammy once. Natural ley magic for the win!

Dare and I step through the doorway to Earth. The moment we're both through, the portal vanishes behind us.

So far, so good.

All of a sudden, Sammy shrinks down to the size of a marble. From there, he rolls up my leg and into the pocket. Who knew that was even an option? Not that I'm complaining. That scepter is a pain to haul around.

Dare and I fly over to the local greenhouse, a spot which I've found to be the most reliable entrance to my father's resting place. Soon we stand before the structure's glass door. Humans mill around inside the greenhouse itself, not that they can see us. Dare and I already cast invisibility spells on our sweet selves.

Once again, I try using my inherent ley magic to open the door. Kneeling down, I reach into the ground.

No ley lines.

I try again.

Nothing.

After five more tries, I accept reality. There's no way around it. I must use the scepter again.

"Sammy, I need you."

The golden marble rolls out of my pocket and up my torso. Once it reaches my hand, Sammy retakes classic scepter form. I point Sammy at the greenhouse door and picture my father inside.

Thin beams of golden light fly out from the scepter's end. The brightness slams into the glass door, transforming it from a clear panel into a portal made of red wood. All the while, the humans inside the greenhouse remain totally oblivious.

Then things go horribly wrong.

Sammy breaks free from my hand to crash through the greenhouse, smashing windows and pushing over potted plants. This destruction can't be hidden from humans. Within seconds, there's a lot of screaming and running away. Finally, Sammy returns to my hand, boomerang style.

"What was that all about?" asks Dare.

I hold up Sammy and glare at him. "Bad scepter."

I've never raised my voice to Sammy before. In response, Sammy melts back into his marble size and rolls back into my pocket.

Dare lifts his brows. "Looks like Sammy's in a time out."

"That he is." Turning, I focus on the red door once more. My heart beats with such force, I wonder if I'll crack a rib.

Come on, Father. Help me.

I yank open the red door. Normally, this is the part where I see my little buddy, Ama the baby Llama, hanging out and waiting for me. He's tiny, cute, pink and has massive eyes.

But Ama isn't here this time.

Odd.

A familiar stone passageway opens before us. Dare and I step inside. The corridor ends in what we fairies call a pocket realm. I built one of these myself and in it, I placed my Castle of Badassdom. I haven't visited that spot in a while, but *meh*. It's always good to have a secret lair ready when you need it.

Dare and I step deeper into this pocket realm, which Mother enchanted to resemble a nighttime forest. Willow trees encircle a large pond. Purple fireflies dance through the air. The grass lies thick beneath my feet. A gentle breeze rustles my hair.

Father rests atop a pallet that's surrounded by pink flowers. Ama lies curled into a nest of flowers at the base of Father's stone bed. The baby llama looks asleep.

As always, King Tristan wears red silk robes. Long white hair hangs to his shoulders. A perfectly trimmed mustache and beard frames his long face.

The prince and I pause beside the pallet. "Father, this is Dare. Dare, this is Tristan."

Dare bows slightly at the waist. "A pleasure to meet you."

I reach into my pocket and pull out the marble-sized Sammy. "So, I was wondering if you'd like to spend a little time with your old friend." I go to move Father's hand so I can set Sammy underneath.

Only Father's hand doesn't move.

Panic streams through me. I've squeezed Tristan's hand before. Not a problem. Now, Father's palm seems attached to his tunic.

I yank harder.

Nothing happens.

Dare steps up next to me. "What's wrong?"

His hand isn't moving. Two words appear in my mind. *Rigor mortis.*

I gasp. Is Father dead? Reaching forward, I set my fingertips against his throat.

There's no pulse.

"This is wrong," I state. "Tristan's not breathing."

Fresh panic streams through my nervous system. Racing over to Ama, I touch the animal's side. "Same thing here."

"I'll take a magical look around." Dare lifts his hand. A sphere of pale light appears above his palm. For a long moment, he stares into the depth of the dancing lights. "There's a glamour spell at work in this pocket realm."

I hug my elbows. "What's under the glamour?"

"Are you sure you want to know?"

There's no question what Dare means here. Glamour spells can hide dead bodies. I consider waiting outside while Dare casts his anti-glamour magic, then dismiss the idea. Whatever's happening to Father, I want to see it first hand.

When I next speak, I force my voice into a calm tone. "Please cast now."

Dare waves his arm. The sphere of pale light splits into two. One orb settles upon my father; the other hovers above Ama. The spheres then burst into a shower of sparkles. Countless particles of brightness tumble onto Tristan and Ama, a motion that reminds me of snow falling.

As the tiny lights settle onto my father and his friend, the pair transform. Flesh tones turn granite dark. Skin firms into impenetrable rock. Clothing becomes stone. One second, I look upon lifelike versions of Tristan and Ama. The next moment, I stare at stone carvings of both my father and his friend. Only now, the pair both have wings, fangs and talons.

My heart sinks. *Someone turned Father and Ama into gargoyles.*

I summon my own sphere of pink magic and tap into Dare's spell. As our magic connects, the scent of lavender fills the air. What looks like blue smoke fills the chamber. This happened once before, when I got a vision of myself standing atop Eidolon Mountain.

Now, the world around me changes again. Dare vanishes. Instead, the Gargoyle King is here. He raises his arms and angles his hands toward Father. A flow of what looks like dark diamonds shoots out from his palms and loops around Tristan. It's as if Father becomes encircled in a winding sheet. The flow of power glows more brightly before fading away. Once the magic is gone, Tristan has vanished as well. The stone replacement of my father is all that remains.

The Gargoyle King turns to me. "Hello, Calla. I can't see you, but can I sense you're near. After all, you are my time traveling wonder."

I bite my lips together, hard. The last thing I want to do here? Say something that confirms where I am. This Gargoyle King is a real nasty piece of business.

"You and I belong together," continues the Gargoyle King. "Come see me at Eidolon Mountain and beg for my help. Otherwise, I can't be held responsible for what happens."

With that, the Gargoyle King stalks over to Ama, grips the tiny animal's throat and twists. The sweet llama falls over, dead. I choke back a sob.

The Gargoyle King then lifts his hands once more. This time, fresh magic pours out. Ama's body vanishes, only to be replaces by a gargoyle replica.

Blue smoke billows around me once more. Lightning flashes within within the indigo haze. When the cloud vanishes, I find myself back in the enchanted forest with the gargoyle statues of my father and Ama. The scent of lavender is gone.

Somewhere along the line, Dare pulled me onto his lap.

"What happened?" I ask.

"You fell over," says Dare. "I caught you."

"I had a vision of the past," I explain. "Mother's ley magic is starting to work inside me."

"What did you see?"

"The Gargoyle King did this. He sent Father away and killed Ama." A memory appears. "The Gargoyle King got upset when I refused him. He said, *you shall witness my power and then come to me, begging for my aid.*" My voice wobbles. "He took Father to show his strength."

"We don't know that for certain."

"No, but Mother will. She controls the threads of time far better than I do."

Dare nods. "Let's go."

What happens next is super surprising, so I'll break it onto its own page.

\- Calla

*D*ear Diary,

Leaving the pocket realm behind, Dare and I step out the greenhouse door once more and enter the human world. Behind us, the greenhouse itself is a total mess. There are no humans around, either, which makes it the perfect place to open another ley door.

I step onto a nearby patch of grass. Reaching into the earth, I grab some ley lines and pull them up from the ground. From here, things should be easy. Once I form the ley lines into a door, I can have that portal open directly into Mother's palace.

Trouble is, Sammy isn't done being a bad scepter.

My little golden buddy rolls out of my pocket, balloons back to his regulation basketball size and proceeds to hop around.

Normally, this would be no big deal. You know, other than the fact that Sammy's activity makes me sleepy. But right now? Sammy slams into my shoulders over and over. His motions make me drop the ley lines before I can mold a door.

For Sammy, this is way aggressive.

I brush the bouncing ball aside. "Not now, Sammy. I need to see Mother."

Once again, I reach into the ground, pull up a ley line ,and try to press the glowing cord into the shape of a door.

Only this time, the ley line snaps. *Huh.* That's never happened before.

I try again. In each case, I get a ley line that breaks before I can make a portal. This happens six times before Dare rests his hand on my shoulder.

"Something interferes with your magic," he states, his voice a low rumble.

"Who? The Gargoyle King?"

"No. I suspect the guilty party is far closer."

Sammy stops boinging against my knee to roll onto the ground before me. Sammy has no eyes, but it seems as if he's looking my way.

I shake my head. "Sammy can't be interfering with my magic."

"Sadly, I fear you have a bit of a blind spot when it comes to your scepter."

Turning from Dare, I refocus on Sammy. "Is this true?"

Sammy flattens out into a oval shape, a form that reminds me of a tall pancake. He half bows up and down, which is his version of nodding.

For some reason, I'm still having a hard time accepting this turn of events. Sammy is too sweet to be a little dick. Best to clarify.

"So you're snapping my ley lines?" I ask.

More nodding.

My heart sinks. "Why?"

A small burst of light emerges from Sammy to congeal into the form of a small butterfly. I've seen that shape before. The hair on my neck stands on end.

It's the same creature I gave to Ivy.

The butterfly wings around in a fluttery circle before falling to the ground like a stone. As the golden butterfly hits the grass, it vanishes in a burst of light.

I gasp. "Oh, no. Something is wrong with Ivy?"

Sammy nods once more.

"Take us to her," commands Dare.

Reaching forward, I brush my fingertips across Sammy's rounded surface. All the while, I picture Ivy's smiling face. Although I barely touch the scepter, a bolt of power whips out. Golden brightness sears into my eyes. When the light is gone, a ley door now appears before us.

As if on cue, the door swings open to reveal the interior of a small cottage.

Dare and I cross the threshold to enter a snug wooden cabin. *Talk about your disaster areas.* All the furniture has been stomped to bits. Bowls of flowers lie smashed on the floor. Watercolors have been torn from the walls. In the scraps of remaining images, it's clear how the original paintings were all of Ivy. This is definitely her home.

I step around in a slow circle. "Did gargoyles do this?"

Dare touches some marks on the wall. "These talon marks are definitely consistent with gargoyles. But it could be other creatures as well."

Oh, no.

Maybe it's Sammy zapping out my power. Or it could be the realization that Ivy is in trouble. Either way, my head gets super woozy. I lean forward, bracing my hands on my knees.

Dare steps closer. "Calla, are you all right?"

"This is terrible. Ivy's too sweet to be dead."

"She's still alive, Calla."

Exhaling, I force myself to stand up straight once more. "Mother will know for certain. Now, I need to see her even more."

Not for the first time, I wish someone other than me could wield the Scepter of Summer. But Dare and I have tried this a ton of times. Only one King or Queen of Summer can get Sammy to do his thing.

I hold out my hand. "Come out, come out, wherever you are."

Sammy rolls out from under a scrap of tablecloth. From there, he scoots up my side and reforms as a scepter in my hand.

Dare moves to stand right before me. "Are you sure about this?"

"I am. Both Father and Ivy could be dying right now." I shiver. "We must see Mother."

"All right," says Dare. "I'll stay right at your side."

I lift the scepter. "Take us to the Ley Queen's palace, Sammy."

Another blue door appears before us. Dare steps forward and pulls on the handle. The portal swings open to reveal a familiar figure standing on the threshold. He's my mother's servant.

I exhale. "Hey, Spaghetti Man." Like always, the guy reminds me of a butler who's created from swirls of blue yarn.

"I am not a Spaghetti Man. I am a ley golem with a name: Octaosirus Ne Regillius Fortesquillarum."

Dare steps up. "Calla and I must see the Ley Queen immediately."

"Humph," says Spaghetti Man. "Her Majesty says Calla may visit tomorrow. *Alone.*"

"Come on, where's my Spaghetti Man pal?" I ask. "You have to take us now."

"No." Spaghetti Man starts to slam the door in our faces. In the past, I might have said something to inspire the Spaghetti Man to change his mind. Right now, I'm too tired to say or do anything. This was a lot of interacting with Sammy. I'm pooped.

Dare swoops into action. He scoops me into his arms and then elbows through the doorway. A second later, we're inside Mother's very blue palace.

"We'll see the Ley Queen now," declares Dare.

Spaghetti Man shakes his head. "I cannot do that."

"I'm a Prince of the Winter Realm. You can't imagine what my magic can do to both you and this place." Dare's voice lowers. "There's a reason the Ley Queen works so hard to keep fae out of her home. Once inside, we can destroy her."

My brows lift. I'd never thought about it before, but Dare and I could really screw with things here.

"Fine," says Spaghetti Man at last. "I'll take you."

"Point the way," says Dare. "I'll carry Calla."

And that's exactly what he does.

- Calla

*D*ear Diary,

Spaghetti Man leads us to one of Mother's work rooms, a blocky chamber made of blue stone. The place is pretty much just a big boxy space with an open pit in its center. Inside that gap, magical blue lines swirl and dive in odd patterns.

The Ley Queen stands beside the ley pit, her body staying still as a statue. Sometimes, Mother goes into what I think of as Blue Fairy mode. It's one of the rare moments when she isn't a regal character, but must another fae.

At other times, my mother is all Ley Queen. In those moments, her gaze stays locked onto the ley pit.

This time, Mother isn't in either mode. Today, the Ley Queen whispers to another figure.

It's me.

Well, not exactly me.

It's Future Me.

There's no mistaking the odd headgear. Plus, I met this version of myself before, back when I was locked into a ley prison. During that disaster, I used my own magic to pull Future Me into my own present time.

Back then, Future Me wore a red blindfold. This time, I can look at myself straight on. A wild gleam shines in my violet eyes. Muscles twitch by my mouth.

Eek. I sure turn out badly. What a strange ranger.

A memory appears. I remember what Future Me once said about the guy who carries me right now.

Dare is far more trouble than he is worth... No matter what he says or does, he will only ever see you as a friend and sister. Protect your heart while you can.

Whatever conversation is happening between Future Me and Mother, I want in. And this is the kind of chat you want to have while being vertical. I focus on Dare. "I can stand now, please."

Dare gingerly sets me onto my feet.

"Hello, Mother. Hey, Me." I gesture to the prince. "This is Dare. He is awesome."

Future Me whispers something to the Ley Queen. With that, this version of myself leaps high into the air. Seems like I'm a pretty good jumper. Future Me then lands right into the ley pit, where she sinks down and vanishes.

Whoa. Jumping into the pit of time threads? Who knew that was even an option?

The Ley Queen turns to me. "Greetings, my daughter." She stares at Dare straight on. "And greetings to the Prince of the Winter Realm. How may I be of service?"

I raise my hand. "I've got an idea. Maybe explain why you

tried keeping me away from your chitchat with Future Me? Something fishy is going on here."

"It is," says Mother simply. "Is there anything else you need?"

Which brings me to a crossroads. I could play this situation a number of ways.

What I Can Do Now

One. Push for the truth about Future Me.
Two. Get details on ley pit jumping. Looks like fun.
Three. Save Ivy and Tristan.
Ding, ding, ding! Number three it is.
Tempting as it is to scold Mother or get time travel tips, there are bigger things at risk here.

"Tristan is gone," I state.

"I have seen this." Mother holds out her hand. A thread of time whips up from the pit to touch her palm. "It is clear. You must go on a quest to find your father. He's being held in a building called Alabaster Hall. It's the Gargoyle's King's palace atop the Eidolon Mountains."

"I had a vision of myself hanging out there." My mouth twists with disgust. "It didn't look like much fun."

The Ley Queen nods. "You must bring both your scepter and Dare. It is the only way to save both your father and Ivy."

"What about the Gargoyle King?" I ask. "Can I trust him at all?"

"You have one week to complete the quest," says Mother.

I smack my lips. "I can't help but notice how you didn't address my *trustworthy question* about the Gargoyle King." I look to Dare. "Did I get an answer?"

"No, but you saw the guy kill a llama. How is his personality a gray area?"

"I don't know. Maybe he's into llama steaks. Gargoyles are omnivores."

Dare fights back a smile. "He is not into steaks. You always seek out the good in people, Calla."

I remember what the Gargoyle King said about the fact that I'm too soft. He offered to take on all my burdens. I guess some little part of me wants that burden-free offer to be true. But is that looking for the good in people… or wanting a Get Out Of Jail Free Card for my sucky life? Something to think about. *Later.*

Mother turns toward the ley pit. "If that is all, I have more work to do."

"Ho, there," I state. "That is *not* all. Let's go back to that only a week thing."

"What about it?" asks Mother.

"Can't I get more time? Alabaster Hall is atop the Eidolon Mountain. It's surrounded by magical null zone. I can't just transport in and out like the rest of the Winter Realm. The winds are too strong to fly. It'll be quite the journey."

"One week is all you have." Her eyes fill with sorrow. "Seven days."

Shock zooms through my nervous system. I haven't known Mother for long, but emotions aren't her thing. For her to get this choked up? It's serious.

"Meaning what?" I ask. "That I die in a week?"

The Ley Queen nods once more. "The same is true for Tristan and Ivy as well."

At this point, Dare loses his ever loving mind. "That can't

be true! You control the very threads of space and time. There must be more time you can allow."

The Ley Queen exhales a shaky breath. "I am pushing the threads as far as they can go. The countdown begins at sunset today."

I raise my hands. "Let me get this straight. Ivy, Tristan and I have a week to live."

"Yes," says Mother.

For some reason, it's easier to focus on all the details of my quest than the whole *you, Ivy and Tristan will die soon* thing.

"And I must take Dare with me."

"Correct. The two of you may be traveling in close quarters, but do not worry. It won't become awkward."

"It will totally become awkward," say Dare and I in unison. We share a smile. Glad to know we have the same definition of *awkward*.

"Well." I rub my palms together. "Looks like I have a lot to do. Thanks, Mother."

That's a good closing line, so I turn and march from the room. Every step takes a huge effort. Still, I'm walking out of the palace like a queen.

Spaghetti Man waits by the same ley door that we used to enter. As Dare and I approach, the portal swings open to reveal my bedroom in the Summer palace. Bonus.

I give Spaghetti Man what I consider to be a very regal nod and step across the threshold. Once Dare and I are inside my room, I check to make sure that the ley door fully vanishes behind us.

Which it does.

And that makes it safe to ball my eyes out.

When I get really weepy, I cast a spell for a crying towel.

That's exactly what I do now. My magical creation is a cute pink square of fabric where I can blow my nose a thousand times without it ever getting sloppy.

Dare retakes his spot on my bed and just listens as I cry. He's like Tristan that way. I move on from weeping to complaining. It helps.

Once again, Dare does that thing where he listens and twiddles my hair. He also casts spells so I eat something and change into my pajamas. That helps even more. I'm a sucker for getting attention in general and from Dare in particular. After a while, I move onto the topic of Dare joining me in my journey to the Alabaster Hall.

"Are you sure you can spend so much time away from the Winter Realm?" I ask. "Saita won't be happy. She likes having you home every night." That's why Mother gave Dare a ley wand, by the way. Saita's a little clingy.

"Do you really think you can keep me away?" asks Dare.

Twiddle

Twiddle.

Twiddle.

The hair play really says it all. "No."

Dare taps the locket at my throat. "Why don't you write in your journal for a while? That always helps you sleep. I'll get us ready for tomorrow's journey."

"Don't you need to go home and get some shut eye as well?"

"I'm not leaving you, Calla."

And he doesn't.

- Calla

DAY EIGHTY-ONE AND A HALF

Dear Diary,

When starting a trek to save the life of your father, Butterfly Babe, and own sweet self, it's important to fake some excitement. With that in mind, I write the following sentence.

Eidolon Mountains, here I come!

Good fake, me.

This morning, I put on my pink battle leathers and heavy boots. Next I add my ermine cloak, which is soft and warm, AKA perfect for the Winter Realm. Doesn't hurt that it's super flattering, either.

Soon Dare and I stand in the Buttercup Forest behind the Summer Palace. Around us, the trees start yapping away. unlike last time, the forest is in a definite *mood.*

"Run away! Oh wait, we can't!"

"Can you give us legs this time?"

"Don't blow up the realm!"

For his part, the prince wears his regular combo of body armor and furs. "We must reach the Articae Horde who lives at the base of the Eidolon Mountains. I have friends there who can help us."

"The Articae Horde? You mean orcs?"

"*Winter* orcs," Dare winks. "Don't worry. They're good people."

"In that case, I can't wait to meet them."

"Are you feeling up to creating a ley door?"

"Sure thing." Kneeling down, I reach into the ground. Right away, I sense the pulse of ley lines in the earth. I grab one and pull up.

And the ley line breaks. So I try another ten times. Same thing happens. I'm a persistent queen, but even I know when to give up. I lean back on my haunches.

"Boo," I declare. "The ley line thing isn't happening. The base camp must be too close to the Eidolon Mountains."

Dare nods. "That's right. The magical null zone."

Rising, I brush my hands off on my thighs. "Can you try your wand?"

"Excellent idea." Dare pulls the ley magic wand from under the folds of his cloak. He lifts the instrument and waves it about. Blue smoke encircles me and Dare. Once the haze vanishes, we should both be at the Articae camp.

The mist disappears... and we're still in the Buttercup Forest.

Curse you, magical null zone.

"The camp isn't far from here," says Dare. "Perhaps we use a more traditional means of transportation?" Long raven-style wings appear along the prince's back.

It takes a few seconds for my sleepy brain to catch on. Not sure I'm back to a hundred percent recovered from my

Sammy-related energy drains. "Oh, you mean we should fly there?"

"Precisely."

"Got it." Closing my eyes, I imagine my own pink wings appearing. There's a tingle along my shoulder blades as they take shape behind me.

I flap them. Normally, this motion would have me lifting from the ground.

This time? Not so much.

Odd.

On a reflex, I turn and check my back. What I see is a shock. My wings look like someone put them through a shredder.

I gasp. "My wings!"

Moving in unison, all the trees twist their trunks and pretend there's something interesting to look at that's *not me.* It's a nice gesture. Meanwhile, my throat tightens with grief.

What a disaster. I'm not even a real fairy anymore. My wings are ruined and it's obvious why. Sammy is draining my life energy. Speaking of my scepter, Sammy is now marble-sized and hanging out in my pocket. Hard to believe that something so small could cause such big problems.

I sniffle and vow not to cry. You'd think after last night I'd be out of tears, but it looks like you'd be wrong.

Dare cups my face in his hands, forcing me to look away from the disaster that once were the cutest pink wings in all of Faerie.

"Things will change over this week," says Dare. "No matter what, we must stay focused on our quest to reach the Eidolon mountains and find King Tristan."

I force my breathing to slow. *Dare is right.* If I freak out about everything that happens, I'll just curl up into a ball and cry. That won't end with me not-dead. "Okay, I can do that."

Words from the Gargoyle King echo through my memory.

At some point, you will fall. We both know you don't have the strength to keep up the fight for long.

Ugh. How did that guy's nastiness get stuck in my brain? And how do I get it out?

Dare leans in even closer. The expression on his face is all things strong and calm. "You will make it to Friday. And once that day hits, you'll return to normal. We won't allow anything else."

His confidence makes me quirk a smile. "*We* won't allow?"

"Never." Dare grins right back. "Remember when we vowed to see a uni-mammoth?"

These creatures are a combination of unicorn and wooly mammoth, only no one had ever seen any in the wild before. Until Dare and I took on the task.

"How could I forget? We were the first to ride them."

"Exactly." Without any preamble, Dare scoops me into his arms.

Side note: I'm spending a lot of time in Dare's arms these days. This is not a bad thing.

As we take off, the trees call out once more.

"*You can do it, Calla!*"

"*Kick butt!*"

"*We still want legs!*"

From here, it's a lot of flying around. Below us, the landscape changes from trees and fields to ice and snow. Along the horizon line, the jagged teeth of a mountain range bite into the sky. One peak juts out above all the others: Eidolon.

Dare keeps up his steady pace. The Eidolon Mountain looms larger.

"We're almost there," Dare whispers.

It's a nice moment. Flying along, safe in Dare's arms. Eidolon is close. A happy thought sparks in my soul. Perhaps this quest will be even easier than the uni-mammoth thing.

In fact, this little interlude is so sweet, I'm going to stop writing right here. Because what happens next is super-awful. I refuse to have it mar the beauty of this particular page.

- Calla

DAY EIGHTY-ONE AND A MEAN QUEEN

Dear Diary,

When we last left my life, I was cuddled in Dare's arms as he and I soared through the skies. It was a sweet time until a massive storm showed up.

Icy air blasts into us, throwing us backward. Snowflakes bite into every inch of my exposed skin. I'm about to suggest casting a spell to get past the storm when I hear it.

A familiar voice.

"DAAAAAAAAAAAARE!"

I know that tone. It's Dare's mother, Queen Saita. This is no ordinary storm. In fact, it's not your standard bad weather of the magical variety, either.

This is Queen Saita's doing.

We're still in her realm, which means her magic is supreme.

Dare shakes his head. "I'm sorry, Calla."

"It's alright," I say. *And I mean it.* Before, I suspected that Dare going on a magical quest would tick off his royal mother. I mean, she lost it when we did that overnight for the uni-mammoth. Can't say I'm shocked that she's making her presence known before we get into a magical null zone.

Dare arcs toward the ground in lazy circles. He's no more excited for this motherly chat than I am. As we lower, the storm lessens, so that's a bonus.

We land on a windswept stretch of snow—nothing but white in every direction. The only breaks in the landscape are the Eidolon Mountain, as well as the imposing figure of Queen Saita. She stands tall as a pillar, her long black hair whipping around her with the wind. Her white gown glitters like it's covered in tiny diamonds. The woman doesn't even wear a scarf and she looks totally comfy. That's what it means to be a winter elf.

I tap Dare's shoulder. "I'd like to stand." Nodding, the prince sets me onto my feet. The moment I'm out of Dare's arms, it feels as if a thousands of chilly pins press into my body at once.

Dare bows his head. "Mother."

Saita narrows her eyes. "Son." She rounds on me. "Calla."

"*Queen* Calla," I correct.

Saita folds her arms over her chest. "So it seems."

"To what do we owe the pleasure of this visit?" asks Dare. "It's rare for you to call in your royal magic and force me to comply."

My brows lift with surprise. *Royal magic?* That's the big stuff. And it means that Saita's been trying to contact Dare for a while, only she's been doing so with standard magic. And Dare has been ignoring her. *Whoa.*

"Calla is stealing you away from me," states Saita. "I do what I must."

"We've been through this before," counters Dare. "I make my own decisions."

"And you choose to help this prankster?" She glares at me. "For years, you've been nothing but comic relief for the *real* rulers of the Summer and Winter realm."

My mouth falls open with shock. Not only is this super-nasty thing to say, but it's also exactly what the Gargoyle King said to me before. What, is the guy sending messages to everyone in the realm with talking points?

"I've known you all my life," I state. "You can be hard to read, but you're rarely mean."

Saita frowns. "Time was, you were a silly stray who lingered around the palace. Now you're risking my son's life. I won't allow it."

Dare's voice lowers to a menacing level. "What do you mean, Mother?"

"That scepter will kill your little pixie. I already lost one son. I won't allow that to happen again."

Dare's fangs and talons extend. It's what happens when he's mega ticked off. "That's enough, Mother. I'm going with Calla."

Saita lifts her chin. "I'm more than your mother. I'm your queen. If I order to you separate yourself from this person, then the magic of the Winter Realm will enforce it. There is nothing you can do to stop me."

Dare's face and tone turn deadly cool. "Even your powers have limits."

Saita tilts her head. "What do you mean?"

"I hereby enact the ancient incantation." Dare raises his hands. An orb of pale power appears above each of his palms as he speaks a spell.

Give me world enough, and time,
Our love together may scale and climb.
We shall sit together and think which way,
To share our future and spend our days.

One orb rises from Dare's right palm. The magical sphere flies through the air to land just above my left hand.

True fact: if this were anyone else but Dare, I would be freaking out right now. Because this orb means I'm about to be hit with a serious spell.

Dare lifts his voice. "Let it be known that I, Prince Darius, do hereby begin the inter-realm courtship ritual with Queen Calla."

I gulp. *Courtship Ritual.* So this is what Dare's been scheming about. *I like.*

The orbs of power flare with white light, then congeal into the form of paper bands that sit on both my ring finger and Dare's. A million questions zoom through my mind.

Can I get some details on this ritual?

What's with the paper?

Is kissing involved?

Saita jumps in before I get a chance to speak. "My son, you can not be serious. This is an ancient and useless rite."

The barest trace of a smile curls Dare's mouth. "Clearly, you didn't expect it."

This is so Dare of Dare.

An inter-realm ritual taps into the energy behind all

Faerie. It overpowers any magic from the Winter Realm alone. This situation feels almost prank-like.

Saita's not giving up, though. She focuses on me once more. "Tear that thing off. You can end the rite at any time."

Holding up my arm, I make a great show of checking out my paper ring. It's just a simple slip of white that loops around my finger. "Nah. I like it."

Dare beams with joy. That's one amazing smile, right there.

Time for a recap.

My Life In This Moment

One. I'm about to be killed by my friend, Sammy the Scepter.

Two. This will be an ugly demise which involves my lovely self exploding.

Three. Death hits me Friday.

Three. Let's not forget that Father and Ivy will die as well, according to Mother. They probably won't explode, but that won't make it suck any less.

Four. Yet my heart soars because Dare just gave me a paper ring.

Sounds about right.

Saita keeps going. "This is nonsense," she announces. "King Tristan must give his blessing to this courtship within seven days of this moment… or else."

"Or else what?" Because I'm dying on Friday. The day is already pretty booked.

Saita's face pulls into what can only be called a grim look

of satisfaction. "Or else you and Dare can never see each other again."

Time To Revise My List

One. I'm going to die.

Two. So are Father and Ivy.

Three. And I'll never see Dare again.

Four. All by Friday.

Five. That is, unless I can climb a massive mountain without magic, find Father, stop myself from exploding, and also get Father to agree to my courtship with Dare.

Six. Plus there are evil gargoyles after me for some reason.

Seven. Also-also, Dare's mother is horrible. She's getting a crap seat at the wedding reception. If I live past Friday, that is.

It's official. Things can't get any worse.

Saita keeps going. "Do not forget, my son. Throughout the whole rite, you must follow all the ancient strictures of courting. And it's all enforced by the magic of the realm. Even I can't change it."

"Strictures?" I echo. That sounds like things just got worse, right there.

Me and my big mouth.

"Believe me," says Dare. "I understand the risks. That changes nothing. I am leaving with Calla, now."

I know that tone from Dare. This is so happening. And honestly? I'm glad. On my own, I might figure out how to reach the top of anti-magic mountain and get back in a week. But with the Prince of the Winter Realm along, my chances are way better.

Saita points at my nose. "What about you? Do you still agree to this?"

I raise my hand. "Count me in."

"You'll regret that decision," says Saita.

"Have you been hanging out with the Gargoyle King?" I ask. "Because he said something like that to me already."

Let the record show that Saita does not reply. Instead, a pair of sparkly white wings appear on her back before Saita flies away.

Good riddance.

With Saita gone, I realize one fact: the moment Dare's mother started howling over an enchanted storm, I'd gotten hyped up on a powerful combination of excitement and dread. With Saita gone, all that's left is a chill.

Make that an arctic level of cold.

The freeze runs deep into my bones, making my toes and hands numb. Horrible things happen to my sinuses.

Dare give me a look. "I'm sure you want to know about the ritual and strictures."

"I do, but not now. C-c-c-c-cold!"

"We can discuss more at base camp." Dare scoops me in his arms. His wings spread out and we retake to the skies.

The Articae Camp isn't far now.

- Calla

DAY EIGHTY-ONE AND THREE QUARTERS

*D*ear Diary,

Dare cuddles me against his chest while his wings pulse in a regular rhythm. As we slice through the clouds, my body feels weightless, warm and protected. Hours pass. My eyes flutter closed. I drift off to sleep.

After a while, my body feels heavy again. The airy sense of flight transforms into the swaying motion of Dare's heavy stride.

I force my eyes open. The sun hangs low in the sky. It's late afternoon. Sunset isn't for hours yet. Works for me.

I peep around. We've landed in a small village that rests on a sheet of frozen water. Large round huts are encased with layers of ice. Wide trails meander through the dwellings. Beyond the village, an ice wall towers up into the clouds. An odd kind of gray light twinkles within its depths. Magic.

And the Articae Horde is everywhere.

I've seen orcs before in the Summer Realm. They're hefty types with tall tusks and bad attitudes. On the other hand, Articae orcs are lean with leathery skin and all-white eyes.

Thin animal skins hang off their bodies. These guys definitely do not look cold.

Now, my mind knows that Dare isn't afraid of the Articae Horde. In fact, the prince believes these guys can help us reach the top of Eidolon Mountain without freezing to death.

That's what *my head* knows.

My heart screams at me to run for it. These are still orcs. I can't help recalling my long history with their kind.

Calla And Summer Orcs

One. They attacked the Ley Queen's castle. Mother knocked them on their collective butts, but still. Not cool.

Two. Let's not forget how they raided the Pixieland Citadel and stomped all the potions to mush. Bilge and Oinky survived by hiding in a cauldron.

Three. Last but not least, Summer Orcs regularly attack the Golden Vale, where they kill fairies and steal stuff.

I shake off my nasty orc thoughts. *Be here now, Calla.*

A tall and gangly orc steps forward. As he steps through the horde, others kneel and bow their heads.

This one must be their leader. Good to know.

Dare throws his arms open. "Ilk!"

The orc grins. "Dare!"

Up close, it's clear how Ilk has a weather beaten face and extra-tall tusks that jut out from his lower lip. His all-white eyes sparkle with intelligence. I try to play it cool, but I might lean a little closer against Dare's chest.

Ilk sighs. "I guess I'm saving your bony ass again."

Dare tilts his head. "I saved yours."

"When we were ten."

Cold air blasts into our small group. It's a reflex for me to cast a heating spell. I summon a sphere of pink magic to hover above my palm. Then I tell that stuff to get me warm already.

The spell doesn't kick in, though. *Yipes, it's cold.*

"Your magic won't work here, oh Queen," says Ilk. He points toward the ice cliff. "That wall marks the mountain's null zone for magic."

I frown. *Bummer.*

"We'll get you warm soon enough," says Dare. "Over the years, the Articae Horde have figured out how to bring in some stored magic. It's only enough to cast a few key spells, like food and warmth, but those are the most important."

I pop my hand out from under my ermine cloak and shoot Dare a quick thumbs-up. My skin instantly feels bitten with cold, so I shove my hand back under covering.

"Indeed," says Ilk. "Our huts are warm. Come to think of it, I have one that might suit you both... If that's acceptable."

My teeth are chattering by this point. "Dare and I sleep together all the time." I roll my eyes. "Wait, that came out wrong. We're in the same room but dressed. Mostly."

Stop talking, Calla.

"Thank you, Ilk," says Dare. "That sounds perfect."

Now, I could ask Dare to set me down, but the guy has serious body warmth working here. And did I mention that it's really cold? It is.

After marching across the icy village, Ilk pauses before a larger hut. It's a dome, like all the others. Up close, I notice how layers of icicles line the hut's exterior, reminding me of the way wax drips down a candle.

The hut's entrance is a heavy flap of leather. Still keeping me in his arms, Dare pushes through this unique doorway.

Inside, the place is simple with rough-cut wooden furniture built on giant proportions. A gray wool rug covers the floor. As seconds pass, fresh waves of warmth surrounds me. I'm still shivering, but at least my teeth aren't chattering. *Progress!*

Dare curls me closer to his chest. "Better?"

"Much." I wiggle a little in his arms. Now that we're out of the cold, the fact that Dare carries me now feels more intimate. For some reason, it gets tough to form decent sentences. "You can… you know…"

"Sure."

Little by little, the prince sets me back onto my feet. As I slide down, I'm hyper-aware of every muscle and ridge on his chest and thighs. Warmth spreads inside me in new and strange ways.

Dare and I end up standing toe to toe with our hands entwined. Ilk marches closer. With every stomp, more ice and snow tumble from his boots and cloak, forming little piles of cold stuff on the wooly carpet.

"You have courtship rings," says Ilk. "Paper level." He grins, which shows off a mouth of jagged teeth. I never thought of an orc as sweet, but this one sure is. "Congratulations."

My face heats. "Thank you."

"What is your quest?" asks Ilk.

"We must reach Alabaster Hall as soon as possible," replies Dare.

Ilk purses his lips. In case you're wondering, Dare and I are still holding hands by this point. It's really distracting.

"How quickly?" asks Ilk. "A few months?"

"More like a few days," I state.

Ilk's grin sags into a frown. "So you must navigate the Eidolon Caves."

Dare nods. "I'm afraid so."

A sense of unease winds through me. "Why am I thinking this is a bad thing?"

"Not bad," says Dare. "Just tricky."

"It would take you months to climb Eidolon by foot," adds Ilk.

"What about flying?" I ask.

"The winds are too strong," replies Ilk. "Even the Gargoyle King doesn't chance it. Still, if you go inside the mountain—meaning through the Eidolon Caves—then you can reach the peak within a few days. The mountain prevents others from casting spells, but do not forget how the caves are filled with their own kind of power. And by that, I mean ghosts and magical boobytraps."

How very much like Faerie. It's one thing on the outside but another inside. I refocus on Ilk. "What do you know about the Gargoyle King?"

"He's a new problem. Gargoyles never gave much trouble before he came along. Good warrior, I'll give him that." Ilk rubs his six fingered hands together. "Do you carry your own magic? Or should we bring you some food?"

Dare cracks a smile. "You know I'm no a fan of orc skibble."

"We raise the finest mega chickens." Ilk chuckles. "You know us. Everything but the *cluck* goes into skibble."

The prince pats his cloak. "I appreciate the offer, but I brought a wand for casting some elf food."

"Of course," says Ilk. "I'd forgotten you'd developed a way to magically store food." Ilk looks to me. "Food and warmth. Remember, that's all the magic that most can bring into the mountain."

"Most?" I ask.

"We have legends that of the rare magic user who can do more. But that is all."

I nod. "Good to know."

"I'll leave you to it then." Ilk pulls open the leather flap and then pauses. "I'll guide you into the Eidolon Caves. Be ready at dawn."

"You don't have to do that," says Dare.

"But I will." Ilk steps out from the hut. Now that I'm warmer, I decide this is the perfect time for a little chat about our courtship ritual.

And since the sun just set, this means I've just started the first part of my seven day countdown. So I'll start a new page to mark my entries. Right now, it's Saturday.

Friday at sunset is my deadline… in more ways than one.

- Calla

ear Diary,
It's after sunset.

I'm in an orc hut.

And I'm alone with Dare.

Mostly.

Sammy rolls out of my pocket and down my leg. So it's really me, Dare and Sammy.

"You're shaking," says Dare.

"It's still pretty cold."

"That I can help with."

Dare struts over to a small box that rests atop a hefty wooden table. Opening the container, the prince pulls out a round blue amulet. I purse my lips, impressed. I've heard that amulets store magic, although I've never seen it in action before.

Dare holds up the amulet in his hand and flexes his fist. A snap sounds as the thing breaks. A moment later, bits of white light cascade from his palm. As the brightness hits the carpet, the power burns deep into the frozen ground.

A small pit appears in the middle of the carpet. I push down the impulse to clap. Mostly because that would involve putting my bare hands back out into the chilly air.

Fire erupts from the just-created hearth. Warmth surrounds me, cuddly as a blanket.

I let out a low whistle. "That's a new one."

Dare looks to me and winks. "Not my first time in an Articae hut."

I speed closer to the fire. Sitting down, I wrap my cloak more tightly around me. Dare sits beside me. As he promised, he brought along a magic wand to cast up dinner. This time it's cashew salad for me, dried fish for him. I eat quickly and shiver the whole time. Despite the magical fire pit, I just can't get warm.

Still, I'm not forgetting my goal of the evening. "We should chat," I state.

Dare waves the wand again, making all the remains of the meal disappear. "Agreed. If you're ready for it."

"Absolutely." For some reason, my shivering gets worse.

Dare opens his arms wide. "Come here and get warm."

No need to offer this twice. Cuddling next to Dare is pleasant in the extreme. I move to settle with my legs across Dare's lap.

"I must begin with an apology," whispers Dare. His voice is deep and yummy.

"Why? You're here." I glance dramatically around the hut. "I don't see anyone else helping me out."

Dare wraps his arms around me. At last, I stop shivering. "I'm sorry about how our courtship ritual began. I'd planned things much differently. I hadn't expected Mother to block me from entering the null zone. That forced the courtship ritual early. It was the only way I could overpower her." He sighs. "You must have questions."

"I've been working on an alphabetized list."

Dare chuckles. "What's A?"

"A is for Actual name of the ritual."

"They're called the Fire Rights." Dare rubs my back in a gentle rhythm. "This means my royal right to try and melt your just-as-royal heart."

I give him the side eye. "B is for Be more specific."

Dare tightens his arms around me. "I fell in love with you when we were nine years old."

"Whoa." A memory appears. "Was it when we went swimming with the talking dolphins?"

Dare nods. "You were nine; I was eleven. I didn't know what my feelings meant. The sensation was frightening." Dare goes on and on about the dolphins and how I sassed off to them like I was a forty-year-old woman. He fell for me like a domino. There's also a lot talk about how pretty I am and stuff. I really should pay more attention.

But Dare said love. LOVE!

My Thoughts On this Momentous Occasion

One. Ha, I totally knew it.

Two. This is both awesome and overwhelming.

Three. For some reason, I'm not getting all gushy right back about the fact that I love him, too. Maybe it's because I'm probably dying on Friday.

Four. More likely, it's because of the *overwhelming* part of item number two. Which means that Dare is right that we need some time for this courtship.

Five. I love-hate the fact that Dare totally called this.

I notice that Dare's been talking for a while about my insult contest with the dolphins—which I totally won, by the way. The prince has now segued back onto relationship topics again. I force myself to focus.

"I didn't know how to handle my feelings," says Dare. "So I convinced myself you were only a friend. Now we've been *only friends* for a long time. But I want to restart things, Calla. That's why I wish to court you."

"Okay, that's really sweet." *And yes, I'm smiling my face off as I say these words.*

"There's a darker side to this as well," adds Dare. "Through all these years, I've carefully kept you away from my world as a ruler. As part of our courtship, you must understand what it's like to lead the Winter Realm. You need to make a fully informed decision."

"So, there's more beyond how Saita can be nasty?"

"Much more." Dare leans over to match my gaze straight on. "Please know that the ring only symbolizes *my* commitment to melt *your* heart. You're expected to meet other people and test your feelings. The spell only shows that my heart is already set."

Suddenly, I can understand how Dare felt all those years ago. Because that's exactly how I feel now. *Overwhelmed.* For some reason, I can only echo his words.

"Your heart is already set?"

Dare nuzzles my neck. "That's what the rings show. As as our courtship continues, these bands will display other things as well. They'll change when our relationship deepens."

"So maybe the paper will read *suck it, winter elves* when I get your court in line?"

Dare smiles. "When I'm with you, anything seems possible."

"Thanks." My tummy gets all twisty. And Dare's mouth looks especially tasty. All of which is a reason to change the subject. "Saita said something about strictures. Let me guess one of them. We need to get Father's blessing."

"Correct."

My eyes widen. "Back at the library, you said there were some obstacles to your scheme. I'm guessing that obstacle was getting Father's blessing even though he's enchanted."

"Correct again. I was looking through ancient records, seeing if there were some way Poppa or Bilge could act in your Father's place. But that would only work if King Tristan were dead."

I tap my chin. "And why do I get the feeling that you still haven't told me the worst stricture?"

Dare shakes his head. "Are my thoughts so easy to read?"

"Only to me."

"You're right. Until I get permission from your father, there can be nothing between us except friendship."

This is one of those moments where it feels like another shoe is about to drop. And in this case, it's not a nice little ballet slipper, but a big old army boot.

"So," I begin. "Lap-sitting is clearly okay."

"It's something friends do to keep warm. All of that is fine under the strictures."

If something's going to drop, I'd rather not wait. So I go for the big question. "What isn't?"

"Naked belly dancing."

"What isn't allowed that I would actually do?"

"Kissing. Certain kinds of touching. Basically, everything that happens after chapter twelve of *Love at Court*."

I can't help but laugh. "I got it." As shoe-drops go, I've had much worse. "And what happens if we mess up?"

Dare raises his hand to show the paper band on his finger. "These will disappear. And we'll never be able to see each other agin."

"And there's the shoe! I knew something terrible was coming. Why couldn't we just pay a fine or something?"

"The magic that protects this ritual is ancient and powerful. People don't call upon it unless one or both courts aren't happy about the union. It makes sense for it to be a tough rite."

"Suppose we get to the Alabaster Hall and Father isn't awake? More of us never seeing each other again?"

"I'm afraid so." Dare holds me so tightly, it gets a little hard to breathe. "Believe me, this wasn't how I pictured this. Circumstances placed us in a bind."

"If I had to do it all over again, I'd still agree."

Dare exhales. "Thank you."

I want to come up with some kind of amazing speech here. There's a lot of good material, starting with the whole *I've loved you since the talking dolphins* thing. I should also say something queenly.

I open my mouth and... yawn.

Maybe speech-time can wait.

Dare kisses my forehead. "You look exhausted. Best for us to rest now. We leave at first light."

"I am tired." I sigh. "But I don't know if I'll rest."

Dare taps the locket hanging around my neck. "Why don't you write in your journal? I'll get things ready for sleep."

"Thanks."

So that brings me to the current moment. I'm catching up on all that's happened. Even after writing it all down, I still wrestle with uncomfortable combination of exhausted and antsy. Maybe drawing Ilk will help.

-Calla

Ilk the Orc

Dear Diary,

When I awaken, the hut is toasty warm. Dare and I get ready, a process that includes munching on some elf wafers. Supposedly these are good for you, but in my opinion they're like eating charcoal.

Dare and I step out of the hut in our battle leathers and respective cloaks. An odd sight greets us.

Hundreds of Articae orcs.

What's odd is how perfectly quiet they are. I always think about orcs as grunting while dragging their knuckles around. But these folks are still and silent. A chilly breeze rustles their stringy hair. All wear dark metal armor. Their tall spears glimmer in the early morning sun in a way that reminds me of so many spikes of ice.

Dare frowns, but there's no anger in the expression. "I thought *you* would guide us, Ilk."

"It's been some time since you entered the Eidolon Caves," says Ilk. "I'm bringing along the Articae Horde." Ilk steps closer to Dare. "For you." He hands Dare a pouch.

Dare opens the leather bag and looks inside. "Amulets." He shakes the pouch. "This is too much."

"Not yet." After raising his arms, Ilk lets out a bone shaking howl.

On the ground before us, long lines open in the icy ground. Snaps echo through the air. The earth breaks as a pair of blue horses rise from the ice covered earth. The creatures are frozen and glimmering, as if their bodies made from shards of frozen water. I take in a shocked breath.

These are crystal selkies—magical horses made from enchanted water. They're lovely and sweet until you notice their clawed hooves and pointed teeth.

"Now." Ilk gestures toward the crystal selkies. "*That* is too much."

I shake my head in disbelief. "You're giving us crystal selkies to ride?"

Ilk shrugs. "You can't fly or run as fast as the horde without help."

A crystal selkie trots over in my direction. It looks at me with large translucent eyes that seem to say, *get on already.*

Gripping the saddle's horn, I haul myself into the horse's back. Not going to lie here. It's a cold saddle. Beside me, Dare does the same on his horse. As the prince settles onto his saddle, he shoots me a resigned grin.

Looks like I'm not the only one who's noticed the chilly ride.

Tilting his head back, Ilk lets out a great cry. The rest of the Articae Horde responds in kind as more ear-piercing screeches slice through the air.

Moving as one unit, the Articae Horde races past us. Ice crackles their pounding boots. Our horses leap into action.

Although our rides gallop forward, they barely keep pace with the orcs.

Our group charges toward the ice wall that surrounds the base camp. The barrier is another wall of ice, save for a thin break at one point. We charge through that opening and into a maze of crevasses. Walls of ice tower on either side of us. The deep ravines continually split into two or three different paths. The horde always knows which way to go.

Hours pass. My butt pretty much freezes solid.

The icy channels open up onto a tundra which ends in yet another ice wall. I exhale. We've reached it—the base of the Eidolon Mountains.

My crystal selkie leaps into the air. A magical force pulls me off the saddle so I land on my feet. At the same time, my crystal selkie touches down to the ground. Then it keeps going, smashing deep into the earth. Within seconds, my ride has completely disappeared. Even the seam in the ice where it entered the ice has vanished.

Dare moves to stand beside me. "Are you all right?"

"Fine, thanks." I scan the mountain before me. The gray wall of ice calls to me. With every passing second, more of the Articae Horde and Dare seem to fade into the background. My mind hits a dreamlike place as I move closer to the mountain's base.

The scent of lavender wafts in the air. This happened back in the library, but that was back the Summer Realm. Here, there's nothing but snow in every direction. I look to Dare. "Do you smell flowers?"

"No," says Dare. "I do sense spellwork, though."

"It's ley magic," I whisper.

Gray shapes move inside the frozen wall of ice. All are humanoid and misty.

Ghosts.

One by one, specters step out from the base of the Eidolon Mountain. The gray, semi-transparent figures wander about, sniffing the air. The scent of ley magic must draw them out into the open. I count ghosts of Articae orcs, winter elves, and even summer sprites. All stare through me and off to the landscape. The dead don't see the living.

Misty cords erupt from the earth. Another reprise from my visions in the Summer Palace library.

These are phantom ley lines.

I turn to Dare. "Are you catching all this?" After all, the last time this happened, I was totally alone.

"I sense something is near," says the prince. "But I see nothing."

Ilk steps forward. "You are part ley elf. Such visions come only to you."

Suddenly, the see-through cords wheel into the air, reminding me of so many snakes being charmed up from their ethereal baskets.

Then they whip toward me.

The misty cords wind through my torso. The sensation feels natural. Painless. Inevitable.

Blue smoke appears. The mists quickly envelop me in an indigo cloud. For a few seconds, flashes of blue lightning appear within the mist.

Then the clouds vanish.

My surroundings change. I still stand before the Eidolon Mountain. Only now, the sky has transformed from early morning to late at night. Seconds ago, I stood near Articae orcs and Dare. Now everyone is gone.

I am alone.

Again, my ley elf side comes to life inside me. Just like my summer elf can sense magic in the air, my ley heritage knows what has happened. Because it happened days ago at the summer palace.

I'm living inside a vision of the past or future. The question is, *which is it?*

A trio of figures stand a few yards ahead. Excitement moves through my nervous system. Two of the people are tall and wrapped in long cloaks with the hoods drawn low. I can't tell anything about their identities. But the third person in the group? I'd know that face anywhere.

It's Ivy.

Cool relief floods through my soul. This must be the recent past. After all, Mother said I must save Ivy as well as Father. They both must be inside the Eidolon Mountain.

I try to move closer. Yet the moment I step forward, fresh clouds of blue appear around me. Again, indigo lightning crackles through the mist.

My shoulders slump. *The vision is ending, and I still have so many questions.*

The hazy blue ley lines uncoil themselves from my torso. Again, there is no pain. If anything, the fact that the ghostly ley lines are leaving feels just as normal as when they entered.

When the last of the phantom ley lines curl away, the blue clouds disappear as well. I return to the present moment outside the Eidolon Mountain. The scent of lavender vanishes. The many ghosts sniff the air, then turn and float-walk back into the mountainside.

I don't know how long I stand there, staring into the ice. At some point, I'm aware that both Dare and Ilk stand behind me.

"The Eidolon ghosts like you," announces Ilk. "They sense your ley magic."

"I saw three figures," I say, my voice low. "One was a young summer elf."

A faraway look takes over Ilk's eyes. "You'll find her."

"Alive?"

"That I can not say," says Ilk.

"You saw Ivy?" Dare asks.

I nod. "I've got a vision like this once before. It happened back at the Summer Palace. That time, I saw myself atop the Eidolon Mountain." I don't add how I looked like death warmed over.

"That's good," says Dare. He shoots me a confident smile. Something warm unfurls inside me.

"My people say there's no sign of gargoyles in the caves," explains Ilk. "You should have a calm crossing."

"That's good." I force a grin.

"It's time to enter," says Ilk. "Wait for my signal." Ilk stalks away. Pausing nearby, the orc leader lets out another roar. The Articae Horde falls into neat lines. They march over to the mountain's base, extend their claws, and dig their hands into the icy wall.

Then they heave.

Great snapping noises crack through the air. A fissure rises up the mountain's base. An opening appears—it's the entrance to the Eidolon Caves.

This is it.

Dare and I step closer to that growing break. We must be

ready to race inside once Ilk gives us the word.

Nearby, the orcs continue to yank on the wall. The fissure grows larger until it's only a few feet wide. Ilk calls in our direction.

"Now!" he cries.

Dare and I race for the caverns. Once we're inside, Ilk's voice sounds again. "Let go!"

The orcs all cry out as they release their grip on the mountain wall.

SLAM!

The outer wall closes. Any sign of the snowy landscape becomes sealed off behind a wall of rock and ice.

- Calla

SUNDAY AND A HALF

*D*ear Diary,

The moment we're inside the Eidolon Caverns, I become aware of one thing.

It's. So. Crazy. Chilly.

How does it keep getting colder? Not sure, but it happens. This time, my teeth chatter so hard, I'm surprised I don't shatter a molar. For his part, Dare doesn't seem to even notice. It's a winter elf thing.

My eyes adjust to the dim light. The cave's interior reminds me of the outside: lots of gray ice with dim figures moving inside the frozen depths.

Dare pauses before a certain stretch of wall. "Here we go," he announces. "See this mark?"

I wrap my cloak more tightly around me and shuffle-walk nearer. A white mark sits on the ice. It looks like a snowflake that's made from spears. "Yup, I see it."

"Orcs come in here. Winter elves as well, although it seems like our entrance has been blocked. Whenever you see this symbol in the ice, you know there's a cache buried nearby."

"Wands?"

"No, orcs bury amulets. Winter elves tend to—*how do I put this?*—reallocate what the horde already set aside."

"That's really sneaky."

"Welcome to my world." Dare raises his hand. His paper ring is visible in the darkening light. "Maybe." He winks.

I stare at the mark closely, making sure I commit it to memory. "I've got the cache marks. What else should I know?"

"You've already seen the ghosts in the ice. There are also some supernatural phenomenon that can kill you."

"Gargoyles?"

"Not as much as you think. I'm thinking more if the ice rapids, avalanches, and quick snow."

"Like quicksand but with snow?"

"Right." Dare scans the icy walls around us. "Ilk and I played in here as kids, back when there was a real entrance." He narrows his eyes. "This way."

Dare and I begin marching.

Then we do a little more marching.

Then marching, marching and marching.

Every so often, we take a break from marching to eat some elf wafers and check for orc caches. Most don't have a lot hidden inside beyond a few broken amulets. At last, we find one with enough furs for us to set up camp.

I order Sammy to make a shovel shape and help Dare uncover the cache. Inside, there's enough stuff for us to make a new fire and set up a few super-comfy piles of sleeping furs. We want to save the amulets from Ilk for emergencies only.

Once everything is all set, I cuddle under my furs and write in my diary. Which brings me to where I am now.

Namely, I'm ready to reset my magical journal into its special locket and catch some shut-eye.

After all the marching today, I don't think it will be a problem.

- Calla

$\mathscr{D}$ear Diary,

By the time I wake up, the amulet fire is toast. It's all I can do to picture one word.

COLD!

My joints seem to be frozen solid. Even my eyelashes get stuck together. It's hard getting my butt out of my furs. All the while, Dare acts all frowny. Turns out, the prince is worried that I'm looking pale and tired.

Which is true, but I'm still not concerned.

Well, I may have an itsy-bitsy bit of anxiety, but not enough to tell Dare about. I make a point to eat an extra-heavy breakfast of elf wafers and even make yummy noises while I chow down.

Dare and I set off on another day of marching. It's slower going than yesterday. I blame the ghosts. They keep popping out of the walls and sniffing around. I wish I could conjure some phantom bells to tie around their necks, just so I could hear them coming.

After hours of them playing supernatural peekaboo, the shock of the undead loses some of its power. At some point, I stop paying attention to the ghosts at all.

That's a big mistake.

- Calla

*D*ear Diary,

We slowly make our way through the caves. By now I've gotten to be a pro at ignoring the ghosts and only focusing on Dare.

That's when it happens. Again.

The lavender scent.

The random, sniffing ghosts appear. These specters are quickly followed by phantom ley lines that burst up from the ground.

Blue smoke rolls in.

The ethereal ley lines enter my *me*.

This time, when the smoke vanishes, I find myself back in the Summer Palace during a big party. This is definitely the past because Protector Lazare is alive and ordering human changelings around.

Again, I'm invisible to people from history, which is fine with me. I stroll through the familiar hallways of the Summer Palace until I recognize a certain head of hair off in a corner.

I'm talking very large coif here. The kind that's only suitable for humans who train tigers and one particular member of the summer elf nobility.

That would be Halcyon.

Yes, Halcyon, the very guy who pretended to be my human friend Griffin. And who tried to murder my father. And-*and* who got killed by Dare in a royal duel.

Only now, Halcyon reclines on a long couch. A bunch of elf commoner girls stand around him, offering to plunk grapes into his mouth or refill his goblet of wine.

And beside Halcyon sits someone who looks a lot like Dare's brother, Reiver.

Okay, it's totally Dare's brother.

I saw murals of Reiver on the walls of my Father's original resting place. The guy is wiry and strong with cropped black hair and spooky blue eyes.

At this point, I could keep meandering around the party, but dang it, this is interesting. It's only recently that I learned how Reiver, Halcyon and Lazare teamed up to try and assassinate my father. Based on how royals can't kill their members of their own realm, it's pretty obvious that Lazare and Halcyon recruited Reiver to do their dirty work. It's enough to make me wonder...

Will I hear their secret plans?

Can I get some details on Father?

It's a stretch, but maybe they'll even share some good info on how to handle Sammy the Scepter?

So I wait by their extremely large lounge chair and wait.

Commoner chicks keep offering grapes and wine. It gets a little monotonous. What about some cheese or something?

For their part, Reiver and Halcyon talk a big game about how powerful they are with magic. Every so often, Lazare or Saita march through the room, dragging away the attention of their groupies. When the girls look back, Halycon and Reiver will have cast glamours to switch places and then act innocent. It's a lot of *no, I was always sitting here* and *are you sure you haven't been drinking too much mead?*

Ha. Ha. No.

This game exists on the same level as the *stop hitting yourself* trick, a popular torture device used by adolescent trolls everywhere. Within minutes, it's clear that Halcyon and Reiver are definitely two things.

Buddies and bullies.

When they run out of magic, the pair pull out some human-style trick mirrors to make the girls think they've moved to another spot across the room. When their groupies move to the new place, Reiver and Halcyon take down the trick mirrors and laugh.

Important note: I lived my life thinking these two were brilliant and remorseless killers. Expert magic users. Fearsome warriors. And the only elves strong enough to take on King Tristan.

Suddenly, it's clear why they didn't kill Father, even though it was three against one.

My Revelation About Father's Attempted Assassination

First. I always knew that Lazare was a loser. After all, I got him to dance the Macarena for three days straight and it wasn't all that hard. So I never expected the so-called Protector of the Summer Realm to actually be a useful participant in the plan to kill Father.

Second. I suspected that Halcyon and Reiver did most of the heavy lifting. This is totally wrong because…

Third. Based on this trip to the past, Halcyon and Reiver are total zeroes. And by this I mean, Jolly the tree naiad has more magic… and the biggest spell Jolly casts is to create a face in his bark while telling folks to *get off his lawn.*

Even worse, Halcyon and Reiver's lameness goes deeper. The pair hang out with common elves—the very types who are too starstruck to see how little power these two have. And then they play unfunny jokes on them for hours on end. Who would have thought royalty would be so immature?

Huh. Maybe my years knowing Dare have made me think all royals are smart, strong in magic, and good fighters. Of course, there's also my personal experience with becoming queen myself. I'm pretty amazing.

Speaking of Dare, a six-year-old flies into the room. It's Baby Dare, black wings and all. Well, not exactly a baby, but the young version is so cute, I just can't stand it. So I'm going with Baby Dare.

"Look at me, Reiver!" Baby Dare soars through the air. In slow loops, he circles the room. Everyone stops to watch. This is some pretty fancy flying for an elder elf, let alone a kid. After a loop-de-loop, Baby Dare sets down on to the floor just before Reiver. The scene is so adorable, I fan my face with my hands.

The moment Baby Dare touches the floor, Reiver goes into action. And not in a pleasant way.

Reiver leaps forward and tackles Baby Dare. It's the kind

of battle move you'd use on a senior level knight, not a six-year-old boy. A huge crack sounds as Baby Dare's head hits the floor. Everyone gasps.

"This is how the big boys wrestle," growls Reiver in Baby Dare's ear. "Never forget you're second best."

Reiver gets up, brushes off his palms, and resets himself onto the couch next to Halcyon. Reiver waves to Baby Dare. "Now get out of here."

A minute ago, Baby Dare had been brimming over with joy. Now his eyes widen with shock before settling into a steely kind of rage.

Anyone who tells you six-year-old kids can't grow up fast never saw Baby Dare with his older brother.

My heart cracks. Every so often, Dare drops a comment about the winter court being nasty. I figured they were bad in the way that living with Poppa and Muti could be a pain. My adopted parents are sweet; they're just incredibly old. Looking back, my biggest problem was being ignored while they napped.

That's not what happened to Dare.

Fresh blue smoke appears, surrounding me in a heavy cloud. More indigo lightning bolts churn within. The ghostly ley lines retract. With that, one thing is clear.

My latest vision of the past is ending.

The blue clouds fade away. I find myself sitting upon Dare's lap. The lavender scent vanishes. All the ghosts meander off. Per usual, it was the smell of flowers that brought them out, not the fact that they could detect me or Dare.

I shake my head. "What happened?"

Dare rubs my back in slow circles. "You collapsed. I

thought you were sick. Then I saw blue patterns on your skin."

"Really? Blue markings?" I let out a long breath. "What I don't know about being a ley elf is a lot."

"What did you see?"

I stiffen. "I saw you as a boy… and Reiver."

"Ah." It's a simple noise, yet when Dare makes it, all the sorrow in the world hides within.

"I'm sorry."

"The Winter Citadel isn't far. We can make camp there."

"Are you sure? That's where…" I don't need to say the rest. The Winter Citadel is where my father was attacked and Reiver was buried.

"It's the only safe place to make camp for miles," says Dare. "Are you ready to go?"

It takes an effort, but I force myself to slide off Dare's lap. My legs feel wobbly beneath me, but they'll hold well enough.

"Yes," I reply. "Let's hit it."

And the marching continues.

- Calla

MONDAY AND THREE QUARTERS

*D*ear Diary,

Dare and I slog through the narrow caves for hours. Every step feels like I'm pushing through waist-deep snow. My breaths come in plumes of frozen mist. I get so focused on moving forward, I don't notice when we reach a wall of interlocked bricks. I've seen this pattern of stone before—it's just like the exterior of the Pixieland Citadel.

Which means we've reached the Winter Citadel.

Where my father fell.

And Reiver is buried.

I shouldn't be curious to look inside, but I am.

There are dozens of Citadels of Learning across Faerie. All are round towers with plenty of space for reading and casting spells. Most have fallen into ruin. The Winter Citadel was blasted apart in the attack on Father.

Lots of explosions in my life.

A wooden door hangs on a single hinge within the citadel wall. It's sealed in place by layers of ice. Dare and I step through and into one of the upper basements. Layers of frost prickle over the walls and ceiling.

I gesture toward the spiral staircase. "What do you think? Up or down?"

Dare knows me well enough to realize what I really mean here. If we march up, we'll reach the space where Father was attacked. Going down will bring us to the lower basements.

"The lower basement is a good place to camp," says Dare. "There's another door there that's opens up on to the caves. Using that as a shortcut, we'll cut a few days off our journey." His mouth thins to a determined line. "Up for me."

"Me, too."

Together we hike the winding staircase. It's strange to walk past the familiar floors in the Pixieland Citadel, only to see piles of broken shelves where the library should be. The potions floor is nothing but overturned cauldrons and shattered vials.

We push through to what should be the third floor. The ceiling is gone—it must have been blown off in the battle. Now the roof is a frozen sheet of ice and snow. Scorch marks darken the walls. A set of overturned tables and chairs sit in the center of the otherwise-empty room. I step over and check out the table. Like everything else, it's covered in layers of ice. Even so, I can see parchments under the frozen water. Large letters sprawl across the top of one sheet, reading Ley Treaty.

Dare stands nearby, staring at a particular stretch of floor. Even now, red colors the ice.

Blood.

I move closer. "That's where you found him."

"Yes." He scans the room. "The place hasn't changed."

Emotions churn across dare's handsome face. Rage. Grief. Determination. "We buried him under the foundations of the building."

I gently rest my hand on Dare's forearm. "We should set up camp."

Dare nods. Together, we march down the staircase until reaching the lowest basement. Since all citadels are the same, this level should hold a ley door that's powered by magical lines. In this chamber, those lines have been pulled out and bricked over. Here, the door only open onto another part of the Eidolon caves.

From the corner of my eye, I spot the brickwork changing. A jolt of shock moves through me. Are those gargoyle faces in the walls? Ilk said that the gargoyles were out of the caves. Has that changed?

I blink again, and the faces are gone. My mind must be playing tricks on me

Dare and I set up camp. We create a small fire put with one of Ilk's amulets. There's no cache of furs here, so we'll need to sleep in our marching clothes. It's not that big of a deal, considering how we'll only be resting here for a few hours.

Our dinner is yet another meal of elf wafers, which suck all the saliva out of your mouth in exactly three-point-two seconds. After our not-so-yummy meal, Dare and I cuddle up by the magical fire.

As I stare into the enchanted flames, my thoughts circle back to what happened today. Seems I'm not alone.

"Sorry about—" Dare and I speak at the same time.

"You first," I offer.

Dare nods. "I wanted to apologize about Reiver."

I grin. "So did I."

"You first," says Dare.

"I told you that I had another one of my ley visions. I saw you as a child. Reiver wasn't exactly a great older brother."

"That's what I wanted to apologize *to you* for. Trust me, I had a plan for introducing you to my family. This wasn't it."

"Don't worry. I'm friends with you. Your family can take a flying leap."

Dare chuckles. "It's a thought at that."

I scan the walls. "I thought I saw gargoyles before."

"As did I."

"Where do you think they are?" No question who *they* are. Gargoyles.

"Waiting," answers Dare. "If I had to guess, they're wearing us down on purpose. He's trying to convince you of something."

"I know. He wants to show me that my job is hard and I should turn everything over to him."

"You're tough, Calla. You'll figure this out."

"Thanks."

Even after our chat is over, I keep picturing Reiver from my journey to the past. I decide to draw Dare's brother. Maybe that will get the guys' face out of my head.

- Calla

Reiver

*D*ear Diary,

An odd sound awakens me. It's something between the noise of ice cracking and a roaring fire.

I force my eyes open.

Around me, the stone walls seem to swirl and blur. A jolt of worry moves down my back.

I blink hard and look again. The illusion is gone.

Dare stands beside me. Every muscle in his body seems taut and alert. The prince nods toward the wall. "Did you see anything?"

"A little." I haul myself to stand. Even this much movement takes a massive effort.

We both stare at the bricks for a time.

Nothing happens.

Crrrrrack.

"I heard that," I state. "Did you?"

Dare nods. "Do you think it's gargoyles?"

I think this through for a moment. "Not likely. When the gargoyles appeared to us in the Pinnacle, they didn't make any noises. It was the same way when they materialized to me on the roof."

"So, not gargoyles." Dare steps around in a slow circle. "Perhaps it was a ghost."

At one time, that statement might have worried me a lot more than it does now.

"Ghosts over gargoyles," I state. "I'll go with that."

Then it happens.

Gargoyle faces press through the brick, silently howling with the effort. Seconds later, two monsters leap out from walls. I decide to call them Fangy Face and Pointy Head—Fangy and Pointy for short.

"Beg us to take you to our king," says Fangy. Although since the gargoyle has such serious dental issues, it sounds more like *bug uth thru take oo thru our ting.* I'd tease Fangy about that, but the gargoyle looks angry enough already.

Still, I tap my chin as if seriously considering Fangy's offer. "The answer is no. Again."

The gargoyles don't waste any time. Fangy swings his great stone arm toward my face. I'm able to duck, but the gargoyle's fist still slams into the stone wall.

And it keeps going.

Boom!

Fangy takes out a huge chunk of granite. Bits of rock go flying everywhere. A light cloud of dust cascades to the floor.

It's pure reflex to reach into my pocket and grab onto the marble-sized Sammy. Pulling out my hand, I raise my arm high.

"I need a weapon, Sammy." In response, my scepter takes the shape of a knobby club.

While I focus on Fangy, Pointy swings both hands at

Dare's head, as if the monster plays cymbals in some kind of gargoyle kill orchestra. Clearly, Pointy wants to crush Dare's skull between his rocky palms.

My breath catches. After a lifetime together, my friendship with Dare cannot end here.

At the last moment, Dare leaps out of the way. Pointy's fists slam into each other. Bits of rock go flying.

Dare and I share a knowing look. The words aren't spoken, but they're out there anyway.

Gargoyles can take down other gargoyles. Even better, Fangy and Pointy stand on opposite sides of the chamber. That gives us options.

"Wimpy knight?" asks Dare.

"You betcha."

Growing up, wimpy knight was one of our favorite games. One bonus of this scheme is that Dare plays the wimpy knight in question.

Sure enough, Dare slumps into a crouch. "Oh, my. I am so scared." It's a good thing that Dare is royalty, because a life in the theater is definitely not happening.

Rushing to his side, I play my part. "You must get up, oh wimpy prince Dare! These clever gargoyles will run at you and crush you to bits!"

By the way, the wimpy knight approach works best when your opponents aren't too bright. Like gargoyles.

From the side of my mouth, I whisper to Sammy. "Get back in my pocket." Every once in a while, Sammy does exactly as I demand. Happily, this is one of those times. He shrinks down to the size of a marble and rolls back into his hiding spot.

"Good job, Sammy," I whisper.

Pointy and Fangy let out great howls while rushing straight toward us. Turns out, gargoyles can haul ass pretty quickly when motivated.

They're ten feet away.

Five.

One.

Dare and I leap to the side. Evidently, I'm not moving quickly enough for the prince, since he grabs me around the waist and rushes me off.

Smash!

Fangy and Pointy slam right into each other. The gargoyles shatter. Bits of rock explode around the room. There might be more to see, but I've just realized the situation I'm in.

I'm on my back with a very big Dare protecting me with his body. We're nose to nose. My squishy stuff presses against his muscly muscles. My blood heats.

Dare's gaze locks onto my mouth. "Looks like we got them," says the prince.

"Yes, we did." I lick my lips. "What are those strictures again?"

"Beyond terrible?" Dare laces his fingers with mine and sets my hands above my head.

I open my mouth, ready to reply. No words come out. So I nod.

"No kisses yet," says Dare. His voice is a low growl.

I'm about to ask if that includes kissing just his chin when it happens. More faces appear in the walls.

"Gargoyles," I whisper.

There's no need to do anything more. Both Dare and I hop back onto our feet. Six more gargoyles pop out of the walls.

Uh oh.

As I scan the gargoyles, more names appear in my mind. I decide to name them Schnoz, Google Eyes, Knuckle Dagger, Bat Face, Spikey Tongue and Claw Boy. *Go me.*

All the gargoyles shout in unison. "Beg for our king's help or die!"

I raise my hand. "I'm standing right here. No need to yell."

They stare at me expectantly.

I look over to Dare. He makes his wings appear as he lets out three short whistles. This is another signal from when we were kids, so I know exactly what the prince is thinking. The staircase entrance sits at the other side of the round chamber. *We can fly out of here.*

Or rather, Dare can fly and I can tag along. You know, until my wings regrow. *I love you, Sammy, but this is an unhealthy relationship.*

Back to the battle.

Dare tilts his head. The question is out there, even if the prince doesn't say it out loud. *Are you up for Free Bird?*

Yes, that's what we named this particular scheme. What can I say? Humans make some good music.

In reply, I give the barest nod. *Good plan.*

Knuckle Dragger steps forward. "Beg to visit our king." He points his massive arm in my direction. "What do you say?"

"Answer's still no."

The gargoyles crouch, ready to attack.

I take what are really subtle side steps so I'm right in front of Dare for an easy *grab and escape* combination.

The gargoyles all rush toward us at once. Dare scoops me into his arms , ready to pull us both into the air.

CRRRRRRRACK!

Long fissures appear in the ceiling.

So many things happen at once, it's hard to keep track. At this sound, the gargoyles all melt vanish back into the wall.

"Ice rapids!"

"Melt and hide!"

At the same time, the ceiling explodes. A column of ice and water rushes through.

Those look like ice rapids, all right.

Twisting, Dare sets me out of the way of the water blast. Instead of striking me, the ice rapids collide into Dare, slamming him against the wall.

Then both the prince and the rapids break through the stone. I gasp, seeing how the ice rapids have cut a hole in the citadel itself. Worry twists through my insides.

Dare is gone!

More of the citadel wall crumbles around the broken piece of wall. I slip through the new opening.

All my focus locks on finding Dare. Ice rapids consume one half of the cave's passage. I scan the fast-moving water, desperate for any sign of the prince. At last, I spy Dare clinging to a craggy bit of wall, barely able to keep his head above the chilly water.

"Dare!" I cry. "Hold on!"

Grinding noises cut through the air. My skin prickles over with awareness as I realize the truth.

The Winter Citadel is collapsing.

Walls crumble in, putting more pressure on the ice rapids.

A wave of water, ice and rock head straight for the prince. The force strikes solidly into Dare, knocking him underwater.

"No!" I cry.

I follow along the ice rapids, keeping pace with the dark form that bobs under the water.

That's Dare. I can't lose him.

- Calla

TUESDAY AND A HALF

Dear Diary,

  I slip-walk through the icy caverns, careful to stay out of the ice rapids while training my eyes on the dark underwater blob that is Dare.

"Sammy, I need you. Now." The golden marble rolls out of my pocket and down my arm. From there, he transforms into his scepter shape. I point him toward the ice rapids. "Set Dare free!"

I can sense magic swirling around within Sammy, but nothing comes out.

Mission un-accomplished.

Stupid null zone.

Stupid Eidolon mountains.

No way will I give up, though.

"Sammy, can you take the shape of a rope and hook?" After all, shape shifting isn't a spell. It's just what Sammy does, just as how elves manifest wings.

In a bit of awesomeness, Sammy changes forms. In my left

hand, I hold loops of golden rope. In my right, there's the heavy hook.

"I need your help here, Sammy. You can roll your round butt anywhere. Now go underwater and hook into Dare. Got me?"

The hook part of Sammy swings back and forth. I'm taking that as a *yes.*

I get as close to the ice rapids as I can risk. Then I toss the hook side of Sammy into the fast moving water. Long seconds tick by. I spy glimmers of gold and dark furs. It seems to take way too long. Has Sammy latched onto Dare?

My answer comes with a great heave as my rope goes taut.

We got Dare, no question

Now comes the part of the plan that I hadn't thought through so well. I, Calla, must haul Dare's butt out of the ice rapids.

It's about as fun as it sounds.

Still, it's surprising what seeing your lifelong crush underwater can do to your ability to pull on a rope. It takes what feels like forever, but I'm able to drag the prince out from under the freeing water.

Soon Dare rests with his back against the icy cave floor. Kneeling beside him, I press my fingers to the prince's throat. *Please, be alive.* The barest pulse moves under my fingertips. I exhale. *Dare made it.*

My next problem becomes abundantly clear. I must get Dare warm, fast. I check the prince's pockets. Does he still have the baggie of amulets from Ilk? Nope. Those got torn off in the ice rapids because *of course they did.*

That means finding a cache of supplies. Fortunately, this is something Dare and I have done together a few times. I rush around the caves until I find the orc symbol. After making Sammy turn into a shovel, I dig in.

Yes!

Under the ice and snow, I find some furs. They're all clean and dry.

But nothing else. No amulets for heat or food.

No.

So I dig deeper. Dare said how the winter elves sometimes hide extra stuff under orc caches. Surely, I can't have hit the only cache in the Eidolon mountains without extra hidden goodies.

Yet that that's exactly what I'm looking at. *Boo.*

Grabbing the furs, I rush back to where I left Dare. The good news is that the ice rapids have moved on, leaving the cavern quiet and peaceful once more. The bad news is how Dare's turning blue.

No time to waste.

There are no amulets for a fire, so we'll have to use body heat.

I can do this.

Nakedness and body heat.

It's for survival.

Not a problem.

Who am I kidding? It's such a problem.

I take off Dare's armor and furs. It's not as sexy as you'd think. That stuff is heavy as boulders, even when it's dry. Happily, I'm a total lady in how I don't peek.

Much.

In short order, I've got us both under the furs. Having a journal means sharing the unvarnished truth.

Yes, I am naked too.

I rub my hands along Dare's arms. "Come on," I urge, "You've got to warm up."

Minutes pass. Dare's skin turns less blue. Some of the worry seeps off my shoulders.

Dare is warming up. That's good.

And with that realization, all the adrenaline vanishes from my system. I can't zonk out, though. What if I break some kind of stricture in my sleep? I'll never see the prince again.

Whatever I do, I won't fall asleep. All of which is why I'm making this diary entry. It will keep me alert. And once I'm done writing, I'll count to a million.

That will definitely keep me awake.

- Calla

*D*ear Diary,
When I open my eyes this morning, tons of things flit through my mind.

My Morning Freak Out

One. Oh, crap.

Two. I fell asleep.

Three. Now it's morning.

Four. Did I mention that Dare and I are naked? We are.

Five. The prince has a nice butt.

Five. And he's naked. I really can't overemphasize that point.

Six. Yipe!

Next I do that thing where I don't really move yet every muscle in my body tenses.

Dare inhales a quick breath. *Oh, no. He woke up.* Next the guy speaks in his low and rumbly voice. And do I notice how I can feel his rumbly voice vibrate from his chest to mine?

Yeah, I do.

My thumb checks for the paper courting ring. *Yup, still there.* So we haven't broken any major rules. *Whew.* I also peek around to see our clothes. They're now frozen right into the floor. *Ugh.*

"Calla, what did you do?" asks Dare.

"You were frozen," I say. And my voice comes out as more of a peep. "You were freezing to death. And you're just my spoon."

"Spoon?"

"Your very muscular back is against my stomach so this doesn't count as sexy time. Plus, our paper rings are fine, so this must be as the same as letting me sit in your lap around a fire, only we're naked and in a cave."

"Calla?" I know this particular tone from Dare. He's trying not to laugh. Definitely not sexy time, then.

"Yes?"

"Thank you for saving my life. However, we need to keep moving."

"Sure. Because of Me. Father. Ivy. We're all in trouble. That's right."

"I'll get up now," announces Dare.

My thoughts are still stuck between the naked globes of butt against my stomach and the firm muscles beneath my fingertips, so I really don't process what Dare means.

The prince stands. And he's naked. I pop my hands over my face because this just keeps getting worse.

"I'll find another cache and some fire amulets."

"Sure," I say while moving my head under the furs.

There are scraping noises as Dare digs around. In all honestly, I assume that's what's happening because I'm still covering my eyes. The guy could be scooping up ice for some snow cones and I wouldn't really know.

The noises goes on for a really long while. I try not to picture naked Dare at work. Not sure I do a great job.

"Found it," announces Dare at last. "Two magic amulets. One for fire the other covers food."

"Can I look now?" I ask.

"Not yet." Dare says something in a low voice. I sense the warmth of a fire. There are also chipping noises as Dare retrieves our clothing from the cavern floor. And he's doing this all naked.

"Aren't you cold?" I ask from the safety of being underneath my furs.

"Winter elf," says the prince. And that's all he says for a while. At some point, Dare shoves my pink leathers under what's now my favorite fur blanket.

"All set," says Dare.

I lower my hands to find that Dare now sports his armor and furs. And a puck of greasy goo sits on the ice before us. That must be orc skibble. Oh well, I need the nourishment. It takes me a few bites to figure out how to push past my gag reflex, but I eventually get the stuff down. Once we're both finished with our meal, Dare replaces the furs in the cache where I found them. I'd offer to help but I'm still tired from dragging his heavy butt around yesterday.

"We'll reach the Alabaster Hall tomorrow," announces Dare. "Ready to go?"

"You know it." I try to stand but get woozy.

"What happened?"

"I tried to use the scepter to get you out of the water."

Dare stands by my side and loops his arm over my shoulder. The extra support keeps me upright.

"In that case, we'll move forward together," says Dare.

And so we do.

- Calla

*D*ear Diary,

The rest of the day involves a lot of hiking through caves with Dare's arm around my shoulders. Because of the odd walking stance, we go a little slower.

Okay, a *lot* slower.

Every so often, Dare says he needs to scope out the path ahead solo. It's a good story, but I know the truth. The prince is giving me an excuse to sit on a block of ice and catch my breath.

No complaints here.

So you know, the icy passages never get wide enough to allow flying, or that would definitely be happening, if only to break up the monotony.

At some point, Dare and I reach another orc mark on the icy walls. The prince digs up a fresh cache of goodies for us. Normally, I'd help. Not this time. It's all I can do to sit against the chilly ice block and stay awake.

Once our camp is set up, I chow down on another meal of

orc skibble. The moment Dare tucks me under the furs, I fall right asleep.

After some quick journaling, obviously.

- Calla

THURSDAY

Dear Diary,

The next day is more of the the same. I keep thinking the same words, over and over.

It's day six.

Tomorrow marks the end of the road for me, Ivy, Tristan and any possible relationship with Dare.

No pressure. Where is this stupid castle anyway?

At last, one of the never ending caves of ice ends in a wall of white stone. Dare and I stand before it, our breath coming out in puffs of icy condensation.

"Is this it?" I ask.

"Yes," replies Dare. "We've reached Alabaster Hall."

Time seems to slow around me. Somewhere, inside this hall, I might find both my father and Ivy. Worry churns through me. Are they safe? I still can't forget what the Gargoyle King did to that innocent llama.

What Could Happen Now

One. We find Father and Ivy within a matter of minutes and—*yay!*—both of them are alive and well. Tristan's still asleep but we somehow wake him up long enough to have him bless the courtship with Dare. Even better, Ivy has brought along a sled for some reason, so we strap Father on and go slipping down the mountainside, singing all the way. The gargoyles do not show up at all.

Two. That's really all I can focus on right now. Number one simply must happen.

Dare and I quickly find a basement entrance to the castle itself. After hiking up what feels like miles of stairs, we reach the castle proper. Alabaster Hall is massive and empty. No gargoyles, no nothing. And it would hard for them to hide, considering how everything is formed from white stone. In fact, it's a lot like the Pinnacle, only in white granite instead of onyx.

The floor plan involves a lot of looping hallways. Every so often, we find a heavy wooden door that opens to a small square chamber.

Nothing is locked.

Everything looks deserted.

Even so, I can't shake the feeling that a thousand eyes stay locked on our every move. I can almost hear the Gargoyle King in my head, asking me the same question.

Ready to give up yet?

The Alabaster Hall has what feels like a thousand hallways and double that number of rooms. Dare and I check door after door, but we can't seem to make a dent in this massive place. Shadows lengthen along the walls and floor. Night is falling.

Tomorrow is Friday.

We check even more rooms. Hours pass. There's still no sign of Father or Ivy.

At some point, I realize that every step is making me hiss in pain. Dare sits beside an obliging stretch of wall and pats the chilly marble floor beside him.

"Come," he says in a soft voice. "Rest for an hour."

"If I close my eyes, you won't wake me up." I raise my hand. "That didn't come out like I thought it would."

Dare tilts his head. He's made it his personal business that I'm safe, warm, and in possession of a full belly. It won't be easy to sideline his rest idea.

"Look," I continue. "Mother said I must find Father. Even now, the sky is lightening. My last day is here. When that sun sets again, something terrible will happen. I won't spend my last hours asleep."

Dare narrows his eyes. "Then sit for a few minutes and write in your journal. Sometimes a break can help you think."

Which is good advice.

Nodding, I plunk down beside Dare and record everything. I even look through old diary entries and draw a bit of Alabaster Hall. No great revelations appear, though.

All the while, I grow more tired and empty. It's a major effort to push my enchanted quill across the paper. Maybe that's because Sammy keeps draining me. Or it could be how with every passing moment, a simple realization looms larger in my mind.

Tomorrow at sunset.

That marks my end.

\- Calla

Alabaster Hall

*D*ear Diary,

After our break, Dare and I decide to split up and check different parts of the hall. After all, we're running out of time and there are too many places left to explore.

Gulp.

As I march through the empty passageways, I can't stop thinking about all the spells I wish I could cast right now. I know a ton of incantations that would pinpoint Father, fast. One thing I don't need is a mapping spell. You don't live your life in the woods and not know how to keep track of wandering paths.

With every passing moment, more panic and exhaustion battle it out inside me. It's like I'm wired with energy and ready to collapse, all at once.

Not fun.

Strange sensations assault me. Is that music playing or the low moan of wind? Are those snowflakes dancing in a beam of light… or the glimmer of hidden eyes in the shadows? My own footfalls frighten me, since my steps seem to sound a lot like the pounding of gargoyles.

Clearly, I need a break.

Not happening.

It's morning now. I have until sunset. Stopping isn't an option.

I turn another corner and gasp.

Gargoyles are here. Tons of them.

This end of the hallway is crammed with massive monsters. Dinky wings, massive arms, backwards-facing knees… this group has it all. I read about this in the library—gargoyles sleep standing up and in groups. Totally true. In fact, they're so still, it's hard to realize they're all alive. The only telltale signs are the occasional ear twitch or flinch of wings.

Gargoyles. I've so had it with them.

I tiptoe away. Not for the first time, I feel like I'm a little mousey who's being led through a maze. The Gargoyle King keeps adding on to the labyrinth, trying to wear me out.

I won't let him win.

As a matter of fact, the Gargoyle King can jump in a human lake. And then he can sink to the bottom until he's covered in old cigarette butts and seaweed. Maybe even some crusty barnacles could grow in his nose, that's how much I curse this creature.

Again, I need to work on my insulting skills.

A figure moves in the shadows, breaking up my thoughts. I freeze in place. Did those gargoyles follow me?

The stranger rushes off; I force myself to keep pace. I catch the sway of a long dark cloak, as well as a body outline that's decidedly male. Whoever this guy is, he's perfectly quiet as he speeds through the passages.

As I rush along behind this man, I try to catch more details. Who is this guy? After all, this mountain is lousy with ghosts. The man appears too solid to be a specter, but then again, I'm pretty out of it.

The man pauses before a stretch of white wall. It looks the same as every other part of Alabaster Hall. Yet something in how he waits sets my nerves on alert. It gets hard to pull enough breath into my lungs.

Suddenly, the stranger's cloak transforms into dark wings.

Like an elf.

No, more than that.

Like Dare.

The man's wings extend and he takes off down the passageway. Within the blink of an eye, the guy has sped off. I'm alone again.

There are two ways things could go now. I could try and chase after the man… or I can check out the wall.

A memory flares into my mind. I picture myself on the roof of the Summer Palace. The Gargoyle King offers me his hand. *Come away with me.* At the time, I was tempted to take him up on his offer. Even so, I refused.

Something about this moment feels similar. I have a choice: chase the stranger or take a closer look at the wall which interested him.

Once again, I refuse the temptation to follow someone else. Instead, I follow my own judgement. Turning, I step up to the stretch of wall and inspect it more closely. The thing is a towering panel of what appears to be solid granite.

I swipe my hands across the chilly stone. Although the wall

looks smooth, it actually feels mottled and rough under my palms.

There's a glamour spell at work here.

Brushing my hands across what feels like rough stone, I search around for what seems like forever. All the while, my ermine cloak sways in the icy breeze. At last, I find the edges of a door. Digging my fingertips around seams, I find a latch.

This would be a lot easier if I could change size. Sadly, my pixie dust still doesn't work on this mountain.

Oh, well. Nothing to it but to bruise my pinky.

Hissing in a breath, I jam my finger into the door seam. Feeling the latch, I arc my pinky around the metal latch and pull.

A gentle click sounds as door opens.

That noise is nothing compared to the panting I'm doing at this point. All I need is a collar and I'd look like a thirsty poodle.

As the door opens a crack, the wall transforms. Where once there seemed to be a smooth sheet of granite, there's now mottled panel of gray rock. Icicles grips down the uneven stone.

Huh. So this entire castle is probably glamoured to look nicer than it is.

A tall door now clearly sits ajar in the center of the wall. Cleary, this is super fishy. This door would be easily opened from the interior. Whoever is inside could escape.

Have I found my father at last?

This is a major deal, so I'm breaking it out onto its own page.

- Calla

*D*ear Dairy,

The door slowly swings opens to reveal a small square room made from what looks like smooth white granite. My heart leaps into my throat.

Ivy and Tristan are here.

Even better, my father's awake and alert.

I've spent hours sitting by Father's bedside in his pocket realm. How many times have I imagined the color of his eyes?

The answer is that they're purple, just like mine.

I soak in every detail of my father. Just like when he was asleep, Father wears red robes. His long face is accented with high cheekbones and a neat *goatee and beard* combo.

I've also pictured his smile a ton. *Huh.* He's not grinning now. *How odd.* This is definitely one of those *happy see you* moments.

Maybe Father doesn't know who I am.

"Hello, King Tristan." I bow quickly. "I'm your daughter, Calla." I grin, trying to encourage some reciprocal smiling action. It's becoming a *thing* with me now.

"Calla." My father repeats my name on a whisper. Clearly, he's overwhelmed with my beauty and brilliance. After all, I found my way to the *frozen back side of nowhere* to rescue him and Ivy.

Speaking of which, I almost forgot about Ivy. She sits beside him, looking less than her regular happy-go-lucky self.

"What's wrong, Ivy?"

She blinks at me as if I'm a walking version of the blight that I banished from Faerie. "How did you get here?"

I roll my eyes. "It wasn't easy, I'll tell you that."

Father rises. He's definitely an imposing guy, and not just because he's tall. King Tristan also works a vibe that says, *I rule and you know it.*

"What are you doing here?" asks Father, his voice deep as thunder. "Go!"

On a side note, I always wondered what my Father's sounded like. Deep and thundery was definitely an option, only the frowning stuff has got to end.

"Hold on a second." I raise my hand, palm forward. "You guys aren't here as prisoners, are you?"

"No," says Ivy. "King Tristan is right. You must leave."

"Look, I need time to adjust here. I just hiked through miles of freezing ice caves while thinking I'm on a rescue mission. And here you guys are, just hanging out." I take in a deep breath and call upon my innate powers of being super-amazing in a crisis.

A moment later, I'm ready.

I focus on Tristan. "How did you get here?"

"You woke me up," he replies.

I narrow my eyes. "I. Woke. You." *Yes, this is taking a long time to process, but it's also a very strange situation.*

"Of course," states Father. "I came here at *your* demand."

My brain still has trouble working through this. "*I* asked you come *here*?"

"That's right." Ivy raises her hand. "You made me tag along, too."

"But Dare and I visited your cottage. It was trashed."

Ivy gasps. "My home has been ruined?"

I wince. "Forget I said that part. And we'll fix it."

Tristan steps closer. "Your orders were very explicit. Only the Gargoyle King may release us safely. Even if you return, we were to send you away."

I hitch my thumb toward the door. "So you could have just walked out of here at any time."

Ivy takes a half-step backward. "Calla, you told us all about this. We must wait here for the Gargoyle King because *you* told us that has to happen."

Tristan folds his arms over his chest. His robe has long loopy sleeves. *Looks comfy.* A random thought hits me. If I live through this, I totally need some Calla-sized versions of those.

I tap my chin. "Do those robes have pockets?" *I'm big on pockets.*

"Calla," says Father. "You're not making any sense."

"True that. I'm a little sleep deprived. And other things."

Father steps so close, he sets his massive pan-sized hands on my shoulders. "Tell me you don't have my scepter. That will drain your mind and kill you."

I lift my brows in surprise. "So hypothetically, if I had the scepter—" and here I glare at Ivy in a way that says, *don't say a word* "—it could drain my energy and my brain?"

"Mind and body are connected. You can't lose one and not

the other." Father stares into my eyes. "Tell me where the scepter is."

For his part, Sammy knows perfectly well that he's the topic of conversation. I swear, he's shivering in my pocket. If I asked him to roll his marble-sized self out, I'm not sure he would.

I set my fists on my hips, because it's a great pose with my ermine cloak. It also says that *everyone needs to be quiet while I talk*. And it works like a charm. Father and Ivy stare at me in shocked silence.

"Here's the deal," I begin. "I'm not ready to have the *Sammy the Scepter conversation* yet. "

Father gasps. "You gave it a name?"

"That's not important now. Before doing anything else, we must nail down how it happened that I'm running around, freeing people from enchanted sleeps and ordering Butterfly Babes without *moi* having any memory of doing this."

Ivy slumps against the wall. "You really don't know."

"Oh, my Calla," moans Father.

I pace in a circle and try to focus. Maybe walking through this whole adventure will help. It all started when the Gargoyle King sent me letters… then I summoned him onto my roof… and after that, I visited Mother.

I freeze mid-step.

More memories appear. I recall Future Me whispering to Mother before jumping into the ley pit. Next I revisit my vision from outside the ice caves. One of those figures with Ivy was definitely my height.

For a moment, it's as if I'm the Ley Queen, winding together lines of information into a larger tapestry.

I round on Father. "Hold on there. When I came to see you… was I wearing odd headgear?"

Father nods. "There were prongy things involved."

I do a snap-n-point move at his face. "Excellent use of *prongy things* in a sentence."

Father shrugs. "I'm a cool king."

I sniffle. *How awesome is that?* Father and I share the same healthy sense of self. *Totally deserved, obviously.*

My joy quickly burns away under some well deserved rage. "That wasn't me who woke you up. It was Future Me."

Ivy's eyes widen as she scooches further away. "Future Me?"

In any case, that's what Ivy says. What she *means* is that I'm nuts.

Father nods. "Calla is quite right. My daughter is part ley elf. Their powers are beyond imagining."

"What else did Future Me tell you?" I ask.

"You were very clear," says Father. "If you came to visit us before the Gargoyle King arrived, then we must send you away."

"We're definitely *not* supposed to kill you," adds Ivy.

"That should be comforting," I begin. "But it's not."

Father gestures to the corner. "I even have a special bag I can throw over your head." Sure enough, a lump of fabric sits in the far corner. *Not okay.*

"Let's recap here," I declare. "First, *I free* Father from an enchanted sleep." And yes, I make little quotation marks with my fingers when saying *I free*. "Second, I take both of you here., tell you to wait for the Gargoyle King, and give you a bag to capture me if I come back early."

Ivy raises her hand. "You also gave us wands for food and clothing. Oh, and there's a *potty wand* too, it's for—"

"I get it," I interrupt. Then I refocus on father. "Yet when I walked through the door, you didn't pop a bag over my head. You told me to run."

A sneaky smile rounds Father's mouth. "I know a little of how your mother's world works. I suspected the girl with the prongy things wasn't from the same timeline as you." He leans forward. "And I like you better."

I scrunch up my face in confusion. I'm definitely not feeling my sharpest, but how could Father have opinions on any version of me?

Some small part of me points out how the shadows are growing longer in the room. I'm burning daylight here.

"Do you know a lot about Mother?" I ask.

Laugh lines crinkle around Father's eyes. It's a good look on him. "I know enough."

"She told me I have to find you. If I did that, I wouldn't die from wielding my scepter."

My fathers face slumps with a look of pure grief. "So you *are* wielding it."

I shrug. "I had to blow up Lazare. Long story."

"I'm sorry Calla. I don't know why your Mother would have said that."

Father then launches into what I consider the Thou Shalt Not list of scepter stuff.

When it comes to the scepter, thou shalt not...

...give it to someone else for safe keeping.

...cast a containment spell on the scepter after the ruler in question has handled it. (Which means the Gargoyle King was lying that he could help me.)

...provide daughters any clues about how to not get blown up at sunset. Evidently, that's not how the scepter works.

I get the list, but to be honest? I'm stuck on the last point.

"You really can't tell me how to use the scepter?" I ask for the fifth time. Repetition is a big theme in my life.

"No, my daughter. I'm so sorry. It truly doesn't work that way."

The floor seems to fall out from under me. Every inch of my body turn numb, and it's not from the cold.

I'm so going to die.

Suddenly, Dare rushes into the room. His eyes are wide with fear. "Calla!"

"What is it?"

A long stone tail whips into the room and loops around Dare's ankles. There's an eyeball on the rounded end. I've seen a tail like before.

On the Gargoyle King.

What happens next is over in seconds. The tail yanks on Dare's feet, pulling the prince onto his belly before dragging him from the room.

The last thing I see is the prince howling in rage as his taloned hands claw along the granite. Dare rips lines through the stone, but it doesn't slow things down, let alone stop him.

Fast as a heartbeat, Dare is gone.

- Calla

FRIDAY AND SOME MORE

*D*ear Diary,

I rush out the door and into the hallway beyond. Nervous energy careens through me as I scan the passage for any sign of Dare.

I don't spot the prince right away, but there's no mistaking how the outer hallway is filled with a new kind of gargoyle. These are all made from marble that's so pale, they could almost be ghosts.

Yet they aren't.

The pale gargoyles thump their clawed feet and let out hungry roars. In the *Good For Me* column, they're all looking in the opposite direction. That's nice.

In the *Holy Crap That's Awful* column, there's the reason why the gargoyle horde is turned away. They're watching their king scale along the walls while keeping his nasty eyeball-tail wrapped around Dare's throat. The prince clutches at his neck, struggling to breathe.

My body shakes with what I think is fear. Only it's not.

Turns out, there's even more to add into the *Holy Crap That's Awful* column.

Tiny particles lift up from the exposed skin on my hands and face. Vibrations move through me, all of them bone deep. My teeth feel like they're about to shimmy out of my jawline. It's some strange stuff.

The truth hits me.

I'm starting to come apart. Explode. Disassemble. Whatever you call it, this is awful. that said, I'm falling apart at a slow rate. Dare has seconds here.

No time to waste.

My thoughts circle back to Ivy. A plan takes shape in my mind.

Even better, it could actually work.

Twisting around, I call into the room. "Ivy, I need you."

She rushes forward. "What is it?" She pauses under the threshold. "There are gargoyles out here."

"I know, Ivy. That's why I need your help."

"This is more regular queen stuff, right?"

I remember how Ivy thought a flash storm and gargoyle party on the roof was queen stuff. But is it, really? Probably not. Would it help to explain that to Ivy right now? Definitely not.

"You're not entirely un-wrong." It's total elf double-speak, and Ivy buys it completely. A sense of guilt wheedles though me. I vow to explain the full truth to Ivy later on. You know, if I survive.

"Okay," says Ivy with a grin. "Do you need me to be the Butterfly Babe?"

"Not this time. My magic won't work inside this place. Believe me, I've tried." I slap on what I hope is a casual face.

"Just run down this hallway and follow it until there's a big kaboom."

"Won't the gargoyles freak out?"

"Yes. That's why you must wave your arms and scream how you'll soon destroy them all. It's like you're a human cowgirl who's herding her gargoyle doggies."

Ivy gives me a look that can only be called uber-trusting. "Okay."

All this time, Father has been waiting nearby. I wave him over.

"Yes, Calla?" asks Tristan.

"Not a lot of time to explain things here. Can you follow Ivy while she stampedes all these gargoyles?"

Father narrows his eyes. "This is a winding corridor. It will loop around to this very spot." Father's frown slowly changes into a grin. Indeed, his smile is a lovely thing. "I think I see your plan." He pats my shoulder. "Excellent thinking. I'll make sure Ivy stays safe."

My gaze locks onto the Gargoyle King, who still crawls across the walls. Dare keeps struggling against the king's tail. Even so, the prince's lips are turning blue.

"You both better go," I urge.

Ivy saunters out into the hallway proper. I'm reminded of the first time I met her. The girl almost flattened some elf nobles just to get the first crack at Cheetos. Now she's marching out to face gargoyles without any drama. *I called it.* Ivy has some serious potential.

Ivy throws up her arms. "I'm Ivy and I shall destroy you! Blah blah blaaaaah!"

Moving in unison, the gargoyle horde turns around to stare at Ivy. The sound of grinding stone echoes through the air. For a long moment, a hundred pale gargoyles simply look upon Ivy. All their mouths fall open, exposing long and deadly fangs.

My stomach sinks. *Why did I think this was a good idea again?*

Spines straighten. Stone arms raise. Claws elongate. The gargoyles tilt their heads back. I've seen this move before. It happened on the roof, right before the gargoyles let out some serious roars. On reflex, I plug my ears.

Noises do come from the gargoyles, only it's not exactly the great howls I heard last time. Instead, they all let out a chorus of screeches suitable for six-year-old human being told she's about to be get cooties.

"Ivy bites!"

"She kills!"

"Flee Alabaster Hall!"

The floor shakes as a hundred massive gargoyles rush away from Ivy. She takes off after them, waving her arms and yelling "Blah, blah, blaaaaah!" at the top of her lungs. Father jogs alongside her, smiling.

While the pale marble horde stomps away, the Gargoyle King keeps pace with them, all while still clinging to the wall. Meanwhile, Dare's face is now turning blue.

Hang on, Dare.

I have another one of those odd thoughts that strike up in a moment of panic. How exactly does the Gargoyle King stay on the wall? None of the other stone dudes are doing that, and with their obvious terror of Ivy, they'd certainly be clawing the walls if it were possible. Is the Gargoyle King hollow or something? Is that also why he can fly?

Focus, Calla.

Shaking my head, I get my thoughts back into the scene. Reaching into my pocket, I pull out the marble-sized Sammy. "Remember that trick mirror we saw in the vision with Halcyon and Reiver?"

Sammy elongates into a small tri-mirror shape. I take that to mean, *Yes, Calla. Your plan is awesome and I'm definitely won't blow you up in a matter of minutes.*

I might be adding a little onto Sammy's thoughts there, but who cares? It makes me feel good. At this point, I need all the warm fuzzies I can find.

I jog along the passage, heading in the opposite direction from the pale marble gargoyles. I whisper to Sammy. "I need you to make a mirror like that, only on a huge scale."

Next I slip back to the spot where I'd first seen the dark granite gargoyles stand in place. They still seem asleep. With silent steps, I tiptoe along the wall until I reach the far side of the horde.

Streams of golden light spill through the hall. I exhale. This spot is perfect. And the colored sunset will hide the fact that Sammy is all golden.

"Go ahead," I urge. Sammy rolls onto the floor. From there, he extends into a massive trick mirror that blocks the rest of the passageway. To the granite gargoyles, it should looks as if there's more hallway instead of a mirror.

All that's left to do is wait for the telltale rumble that means the dark granite gargoyles are on their way. Sure enough, the floor shakes. Far-off screeches sound.

Next I need to get my own horde moving in the right direction. And by *right*, I mean running straight for the horde that Ivy is making stampede. It's a careful calculation of how fast I think the granite horde can run, the speed that Ivy's horde is going, and when I need to tell Sammy to stop being a trick mirror.

In other words, it's a big ass guess on my part.

The floor shimmies with more force. Distant rumbles sound from Ivy's horde. Time to get my own gargoyles going.

I slip onto the opposite side of the trick mirror. From this spot, I can watch both hordes, yet none of them can see me. Once I'm safely hidden, I cup my hands by my mouth. "Hey guys! The Gargoyle King wears army boots!"

None of the gargoyles flinch, let alone run.

"Get moving, you blockheads!"

Still no reaction. That may have been too Charlie Brown for this group.

I decide to return to the classics. "You're ugly and your mother dresses you funny!"

That gets them. Moving in one long line, my gargoyle horde races toward me and my Sammy-mirror. At the same time, Ivy drives the pale granite gargoyles from the opposite direction. Her horde also stretches across the hallway in single file. If this works out, the two hordes will slam into each other, one on one, and make a big ass mess.

Love it.

The Gargoyle King is not a fan of the situation. He howls to his hordes. "Stop! Halt! Heed me, your king!"

Both hordes pay zero attention. *Heh heh heh.*

I set my pinkies at either edge of my mouth and let out three short whistles. This is a classic signal between me and Dare. It means we need to enact our infamous Free Bird plan, AKA the same one we almost used in the Winter Citadel basement. If it works, Dare will fly away at the last second.

Please, let it work.

I stay plastered against the wall, watching as the two gargoyle hordes rush straight for each other. They keep running and howling. Neither group knows they head to the other, all thanks to Sammy's illusion.

They're fifty yards apart.

Twenty.

Ten.

Five.

One.

"Now, Sammy!" I cry. Instantly, Sammy returns to his marble shape.

Crash!

The two hordes run slap-bang into each other. Bits of rubble fly into the air. At the same time, the Gargoyle King winces.

It's just the opportunity Dare needs.

The prince extends his wings and flies right out from under the tail's hold. Dare soars through the air. The Gargoyle King extends his wings and follows close behind.

I cheer. The gargoyles now lie in pieces on the floor. Sammy is safe. Dare is flying away. I can't see Ivy and Tristan, but there's a lot of stone dust in the air. I'm sure they're both somewhere nearby, safe and sound.

I exhale. *They're all safe.*

Suddenly, invisible knifes cut through my body. Particles fly up from my skin. This is the same as what happened before, only now my clothes are disintegrating as well. Hissing in a pained breath, I crumple to my knees.

Dare lands at my side. Tristan and Ivy stand nearby.

"What's happening?" asks Dare. "You found your father. Any threat from the scepter should be gone."

"I don't know," I state. My voice comes out low and rough. "Father can't tell me, either."

The Gargoyle King hovers above us, his wings beating in a steady rhythm. If he's upset about losing two hordes of his followers, then the king doesn't show it. Not for the first time, I really wish I could cast a spell.

"I can help you." The Gargoyle King extends his arms. "Only I can save you."

Tristan glares at the king. "Don't lie to my daughter." Still, a question lingers in my father's eyes. Tristan could sprout wings and take on the Gargoyle King. Yet he doesn't. I haven't known my father for long, but I remember how Tristan didn't bag me up when I first entered his room. Father likes to keep his options open.

Which means Tristan isn't sure if the Gargoyle King can really help me or not.

That makes two of us.

Despite the pain, I force myself to stand. This is yet another one of those conversations that's best to have while vertical. Once I'm upright, I focus on the Gargoyle King once more. "Still not begging for your help," I declare.

"It has been so hard to put you through this," continues the king. "I've been forced to watch while you slowly make your way here, when simply accepting my help would have been so much easier."

"What's your point?" I ask.

"By now, you must see how hard it is to rule," says the king. "I can help you."

"Prove it," states Dare. It's a tribute to the prince that even though he was almost killed by the Gargoyle King, he's willing to do anything to keep me unexploded.

"With ease," says the king. "You've seen how no one is powerful enough to cast even minor spells here."

"Sure," I state.

The Gargoyle King raises his arms. A blast of snow white power erupts from his palms to slam into what remains of his gargoyle horde. The many piles of rubble are turned into so much dust. "Does anyone doubt my powers now?"

Much as I hate to admit it, that was impressive. I've been thrilled to have an amulet make me some orc goop, let alone transform rocks to dust. Plus, there are a ton of glamour spells on this palace. That takes some serious power to conjure.

"I am your only choice," continues the Gargoyle King. "I'd hoped to make you see this in a gentle way, but that didn't happen. Now you've had days to feel the draining power of the scepter. You've seen how your precious prince fails to protect himself from the dangers of the Eidolon Mountain... imagine the sad assistance he could provide across the entire realm."

"Leave her alone," snarls Dare.

"This is Calla's choice." The Gargoyle King announces. "If anyone interferes, you'll be next to die."

Knife-stabbing hurt sears into my body. More particles fly up from my skin. My thoughts swirl. *I'm so tired.* This has all been one long torture to break my spirit. And Future Me has been in cahoots here. Does that mean this is actually a good deal? I don't want to get stuck with that dumb headgear.

The Gargoyle King extends his arms in my direction once more. "Come away with me. I can make all your worries vanish."

Despite the hurt, threads of facts appear in my mind. With

every passing second, they weave into a larger tapestry. A rough outline of a greater image appears. Suppose Mother had a plan, but it wasn't what I expected?

Perhaps my quest wasn't just to find Tristan, but to share in a journey to reach this spot? Maybe I'm supposed to learn something entirely different. I carefully scan the Gargoyle King.

Fresh threads of memory appear. This king climbs walls when no other gargoyle can manage it... he uses the same words as Saita... casts so many glamour spells... and has such searing blue eyes.

At last, the details of the picture become clear.

Mother, you're brilliant.

I refocus on the Gargoyle King. "In one way, you are absolutely right. You're the one who I've been searching for all along."

The next part is so awesome, it gets a new page.

- Calla

FRIDAY AND EVEN MORE

*D*ear Diary,

When we last visited my life, I brilliantly destroyed two hordes of gargoyles without so much a chipping a nail.

Now I must deal with the Gargoyle King.

This will be tougher.

The king raises his arms. "It's true that you haven't begged *yet*, Calla." He points his palms toward Dare. "The prince has no weapons. No magic can protect him. And I can destroy him in a moment."

Ivy and Father rush toward me. I appreciate the attempt at back-up, but I won't risk any more lives. "Please stay back," I whisper.

Ivy freezes in place. It's the queen-thing I have going. She does as ordered. Father pauses and tilts his head. His eyes narrow in a way that says, *are you sure?*

I muster up my most confident voice. "I've got this, Father."

Which is a pile of uni-mammoth poop. Still, I pull it off. Father stays put.

For his part, Dare steps to my side and laces his fingers with mine. I open my mouth, ready to tell him to stand back as well.

"I trust you," says Dare in his deep and growly voice. "I trust *us.*"

I shut my yap. *What a sweet thing to say.* At this point, there's no way I'm telling Dare to step away. Plus, I do feel better while holding the prince's hand.

Dare's touch gives me the strength to focus on the Gargoyle King once more. "Here's what will happen next," I announce. "You'll lower your arms and go quietly to the dungeons of the winter realm."

A slow smile rounds the Gargoyle King's mouth. "And why would I do that?"

Here it comes.

"Because I know who you are." I add a dramatic pause because I'm queen and this is my revelation. "Reiver."

A flash of panic shines in the Gargoyle King's eyes, but he hides it quickly. Not fast enough, though. I totally caught the fear.

"No," says Guy Who Is Totally Reiver. "I am the Gargoyle King. And you've always held my heart."

I point to my face. "This is me, not believing you one bit. Where were you when I was an unknown pixie? I don't meet you until I become queen… when you pull some serious stalker behavior to convince me to come away with you. Plus, who tortures someone they care about in order to convince them to do anything? If that's your version of affection, you can stick it."

"Come away with me, Calla." Guy Who Is Reiver flexes his palms again. "Or I'll use my superior magic to kill everyone you love. This is for your own good."

My throat tightens with worry. *Am I doing the right thing? Could Reiver really be powerful enough to kill Dare?* I glance over to the prince. Dare's face betrays no trace of emotion. Still, he gives my hand a gentle squeeze. I know what that means.

Dare still believes in me.

On my free hand, I run my thumb over the paper ring Dare gave me seven days and a thousand years ago. The touch of the band provides more strength.

It all comes down to this. I'm about ninety percent sure Reiver isn't all that powerful in magic.

Eighty.

Okay, I'm a percentage of sure.

I need Reiver The Gargoyle to drop the whole *I'm a superpowerful sorcerer* act. To that end, it's best if I push forward here. And if I'm wrong? I'll deal with that later.

I nod once to myself. *Good plan, Calla.*

With my decision made, I focus on the guy who (I hope) has no magic. "I saw the truth of your history, Reiver. You learned all sorts of glamour tricks from Halcyon. As a matter of fact, his whole palace is one big illusion."

Let the record show that the Gargoyle King does not seem impressed. In fact, I'm not even sure he's paying attention anymore. If he didn't have his arms raised, I'd think the Gargoyle King was napping. So I keep pushing.

"Also, your powers are crap. That's why you want to *help me*." When I say the words *help me*, I make little finger quotes with my free hand. "I'm the one who wields true power. All you have is show and no substance."

The Gargoyle King tilts back his head and lets out bone-chilling a roar. Ivy shivers. Even Father pales. Dare keeps his steady grip on my hand.

The last threads of truth fall into place.

"You're not wielding your own power, are you? It's mine. Somehow, you hustled me in another reality."

"Don't press me," says the Gargoyle King. "I will destroy Dare."

"Sha. You can't kill your own brother, at least not directly. You didn't even order your gargoyles to attack him. What's that about? Saita told you not to?"

The Gargoyle King lets out another great howl. "I am not Reiver!"

Dare releases my hand and moves to stand between me and the Gargoyle King. "I believe Calla."

My chest suddenly feels so light, it's like my wings are back and I'm flying. A protective Dare is a swoon-worthy Dare.

The Gargoyle King twists his face into a snarl. "Calla's about to implode with power she doesn't understand. Do not stop me from saving her life."

When Dare next speaks, his voice is low with menace. "I challenge you to a duel, brother."

"No," snarls the Gargoyle King.

"You can not ignore the power of the realm," says Dare. "The magic will force you into battle." Dare tosses his cloak aside. "Did you know Halcyon and I fought a royal duel? That's how I killed him."

The Gargoyle King's eyes flare with rage. "You killed Halcyon?" He swipes his massive arm toward Dare. I'm no expert warrior, but the Gargoyle King's movement says he plans to knock Dare's head clean off.

But can he do it?

I've seen the power of gargoyle strikes. Back in the Winter Citadel, they punched through the walls with such force, the entire structure fell in.

Dare raises his arm and blocks the blow. That's right. Dare's hand clasps the gargoyle's massive fist, stopping all the king's momentum.

My breath catches. It's one thing to suspect a massive gargoyle is really a big phony. It's another deal to watch your maybe-boyfriend to fight the creature with ease.

Dare twists the Gargoyle King's arm. "Fight me without glamours, Reiver."

The Gargoyle King raises his free hand. An amulet gleams in his claw. The king tightens his grip, destroying the amulet and whatever magic is held inside. A flare of white light erupts from his palm. As the brightness fades, the appearance of the Gargoyle King changes.

He transforms into Dare's supposedly-dead brother, Reiver.

"I watched when you found my body," says Reiver. Dare's brother looks the same as always—a wiry man with short hair and a searing gaze. "How you wept over what you *thought* was my corpse. You actually cried for another elf that I'd placed under a glamour spell. You and mother buried that fool alive."

With that, Reiver pounces on Dare. The fight moves so quickly, it's hard to keep track. Punches are thrown and blocked. At one point, Reiver gets chucked against the wall. Dare takes an elbow to the throat.

It's nerve wracking that no one can step in and help. Especially considering how I had a few chances to trip Reiver when no one was looking.

At last, Dare pins Reiver to the floor. "This is how men wrestle," growls Dare. "We choose a fair fight."

Although Reiver's face is pinned to the floor, there's no missing the evil gleam in his eyes. Dare's brother has something planned, that's for sure.

Reiver grips a new amulet in his palm. Even worse, the item has Future Me's face on it. The sight makes my stomach churn. Future Me conjured up something to help Reiver. I don't even want to know what else she's been up to.

I'm so the better me.

"Watch out!" I cry. "Reiver's got an amulet."

Dare reaches for his brother's hand, but he's not fast enough. Reiver clenches the amulet tightly in his fist. The magical item snaps, sending blue sparks into the air.

The sight makes my blood heat with anger. Blue magic is ley power. That's *my* energy Reiver's stealing.

Crack!

Long fissures appear in the ceiling. My heart sinks. I've seen this show before. Don't want another set of tickets.

"Ice rapids!" I call.

The ceiling break open. Freezing water shoots toward Dare. This puts the prince in a tough spot: does he release Reiver or avoid the icy blast? At the last moment, Dare twists his body, setting Reiver right into the pull impact of the spray.

Looks like Dare chose the best of both worlds, really.

The ice rapids push Reiver straight into the wall. Just as it happened in the Winter Citadel, the stone barrier doesn't stop the freezing water. The ice rapids break through the wall and wash down the mountainside, taking Reiver along for the ride.

I walk up to the new opening. Dare stays by my side. "Do you think he'll drown?" I ask.

Dare frowns. "I doubt we'd be that lucky."

Tristan approaches as well. "I lived through an assassination attempt and enchanted sleep," states Father. "I swear, watching that scene came far closer to killing me."

Ivy rushes up to join us. "We did it!"

Next thing I know, I'm sharing a big hug with Dare, Ivy and Father. Dare's strong arms hold me close. Tristan rests his chin atop my head. And Ivy holds on from the other side.

The truth slowly sinks in. Ivy is right. We really did it.

Suddenly, every bone in my body starts to vibrate with more force. Particles of me break free from me faster than ever. Stabbing pain erupts behind my eyes and in my stomach.

Ivy isn't the only one who's right. Mother's prediction is coming true as well.

I'm breaking apart, piece by piece.

- Calla

*D*ear Diary,
   So this sucks.

Everyone steps back as particles rise up from my skin and clothes. The tiny bits of me spin around like so many moons to my star.

"What can I do?" asks Dare, but his voice sounds a million miles away.

A blast of chilly wind grabs my attention. Turning, I face the huge break in the wall again. More freezing gusts blast against my skin. Looking down, I scan the snow-covered mountainside. The dying sun casts long shadows on the crags and ridges below. From this angle, all the ghostly faces appear upside down.

With a gasp, I realize the truth. This is the moment from my first vision, way back at the Summer Palace. Now I'm here. And yes, I really don't look too good.

Raising my hand, I watch as more particles lift up from my fingers. The sensation is like thousands of tiny knives cutting into me. I've been so afraid of this happening, and yet here it is.

A realization envelops every corner of my soul. I was so certain that I needed to find father, but I was wrong. What I truly needed to do was discover Reiver's identity.

Perhaps that's happening again.

What if falling apart isn't really the problem?

More particles fly up from my body. I sense every bit of power as it flies away. More hurt radiates through my body. I look to Dare. The lines of his handsome face are pulled tight with panic.

When I next speak, my voice breaks, and it's not from emotion. My throat is coming apart. "Life blows us apart," I begin. "I started as a faeling pixie. Now I'm an elf queen. There was no way to stop that."

Every ounce of Dare's focus is trained on me. "What are you saying, Calla?"

"I've been thinking about this the wrong way. The trick isn't finding some way to avoid destruction. No, the challenge is…" My voice gives out.

"…How to reform yourself once more," finishes Dare.

I force myself to nod. A sense of satisfaction winds through me. My prince understands. We share a long look filled with fear and hope.Without saying another word, I'm certain we both realize the risk here.

In life, it's never a guarantee that you'll reform properly, or at all. Still, that's what I must do.

The last of the sun passes behind the horizon line. Once darkness fully descends, I explode. All the particles in my body break free. Pain sears through every corner of my consciousness.

I scream with all my might, yet do not make a sound.

My thoughts shatter only to congeal again inside what appears to be a long blue corridor. There's no question in my mind—I now stand inside a ley line. Future Me waits a few yards away. There's still that strange tick by her eye and the odd choice of headwear. Longing shines in her version of my violet eyes. She reaches for me, arm outstretched.

Invisible threads of connection flow between us. She is me and not, all at once. And she's hurting. I raise my arm, my own hand straining to take hers.

"Come away with me," she whispers.

I stumble a half-step backward. *Come away with me.* That's exactly what Reiver said as the Gargoyle King. Future Me may be hurting, but then again so was that rabid squirrel who took up residence in Jolly last summer. The thing almost bit my finger off.

I lower my arm. "No."

My consciousness pulls back from the interior of the ley line. I'm aware of standing inside the Alabaster Hall once more, only I have no form.

Ghosts are everywhere. Elf women and children. Articae orcs. Hobgoblins and pixies. Some are well dressed and plump, others look are just skin and bone. All stare at me with questioning looks.

Somehow I am one of them, only I am not dead.

With sheer will, I summon the parts of me back together. Blue smoke rolls in from the skies, the essence of my ley power. Piece by piece, I retake my shape. Every molecule returns, starting with my skeleton. Muscles layer upon my frame. Skin envelops me, along with a new set of wings and clothing.

I become whole once more.

Blinking, I look examine myself again. I'm back to being me, only with pink robes.

Before me, there stands Dare, Ivy and Tristan. All three fall down onto their knees. The icy wind still churns around us, but only Ivy and Tristan shiver under the chill.

The prince's gaze meets mine. "You did it," he whispers, his voice rough.

I wink. "Hey, I had some help."

My hand stings. Looking down, I find tendrils of white smoke entwining around my left hand. The paper ring that marks our courtship ritual curls.

It's dying.

Shock zings through my limbs. I'd forgotten about those crazy strictures. Dare and I needed Father's approval for our courtship by sunset today... or we can never see each other again.

- Calla

FRIDAY JUST WON'T END

*D*ear Diary,
Now is a great time for a little recap of my to do list over the last seven days.

My Crap Week

One. Find Father by Friday so he doesn't die. *Done.*

Two. Ivy. Same deal. *Also done.*

Three. Avoid getting blown up. Turns out, this was some sketchy stuff from my time-traveling mother. The trick was to accept that I had to explode, so I did. *Still counting that as a win.*

Four. Now I'm about to be permanently separated from Dare because I'm a queen, he's royal, and we're stuck in this cuckoo courtship ritual.

More pale smoke twists around my hand. Bits of the white paper ring tumble to the ground.

Lift my hand, I turn to Dare. It's been one big magilla of a day. All I can manage is a single word. "No."

Dare rounds on Tristan. "I have requested the ancient

courtship ritual with your daughter." He cups my ring hand in his palms. "Now we humbly request your blessing."

Father nods. "Given."

The white smoke on my hand flares with an ethereal light. When the brightness fades, my paper rings is now made from braided twine. The same is true for Dare's band as well.

Twine. That's more solid than paper. Seems like a good sign. Looking to Dare, I find he's positively beaming with joy.

Definitely a good sign.

Father sets his hand on my shoulder. "So you know, I would normally have asked your opinion on the subject, but I already know your heart. You've spoken to me often of Dare."

A chill crawls down my back. "You mean, all those times I hung out in your forest and talked, you could hear me?"

"Every word." Father winks. "Where do you think I learned the phrase *prongy things* to describe the hair stylings of your future self? You told me all about meeting her."

My eyes widen so large, I'm surprised they don't pop out of my head. "And you heard that, too?"

"I did and enjoyed every moment. You're a wonderful daughter." Father opens arms wide.

Don't need to think twice about this situation. I fall right into a mega hug with Tristan. Of all the things I expect to happen on this mountaintop, sharing so many hugs with Father was not on the list.

No complaints, though.

Breaking our embrace, I turn to Dare. He makes a great show of checking out a nearby chunk of stone. I frown. I was really hoping to continue the hug-a-thon and Dare was my next target. And I know the prince.

Dare is not a rock person. He's totally pretending to check out those stones.

Oh, well. His loss.

I call out to the general group because Dare is clearly busy right now. "Who's ready to climb down the mountain? I feel like a million bucks." Shaking my shoulders, I make my wings reappear. "Even better, we can fly."

A gust of wind blasts through the missing wall. I shiver. "Oh right. Flying is not an option." I tap my cheek and consider things. "On second thought, how about those caves?"

And that's exactly where we go.

\- Calla

DAY EIGHTY-NINE

D ear Diary,

It's been three days in the ice caves. We're making great time. Turns out, it totally helps that I can walk on my own and everything.

So that's good.

Now for the crappy part: Dare keeps ignoring me. Talk about irritating in the extreme. I have his string ring now. There are big things we must discuss such as, *what's with the string?* And I'm sure there's other stuff I could list, only I can't focus because I'm too ticked off at being ignored. But whenever I approach Dare, he keeps turning away to look at ice formations.

Fine. Dare needs some space. I don't care.

For her part, Ivy listens as Father asks me questions. For a guy who looked asleep, it's almost as if he was taking notes.

Tristan's Borderline-Embarrassing Questions

Question from Father: What did I do when I attended human high school?

My answer: Tackle mean girls.

Father: Why did I consider kissing Griffin? (By the way, Dare growled when this question was asked. *Heh heh heh.*)

Me: I considered kissing Griff because he was so kind and attentive.

Father: Do I really primp before every visit from Dare?

Me: Maybe.

By the way, this final question positively ruined my Griffin-kiss story. The moment Father asked it, Dare began smirking while continuing to ignore me.

All in all, I learned a key lesson. Father has a memory like a steel trap. From now on, I share as little as possible.

- Calla

DAY NINETY

Dear Diary,
     More hiking.
More ignoring of *moi* by Dare.
We are not amused.
Again.
- Calla

DAY NINETY-ONE

$\mathcal{D}$ear Diary,

This journal entry is NOT about how Dare isn't paying me enough attention. Instead, I'm writing about all the great things I've learned about other people in this hiking party.

New Things I Learned

Dare. Nothing. Unless you count that he's developed an unhealthy interest in ice formations.

Ivy. She's okay with her cottage being ruined if I can rebuild it better. This won't be a problem as I have ideas.

Tristan. Really likes to ask embarrassing questions. I think he's verbally pranking me.

As the days pass, the caves become slightly warmer. Dare thinks that we'll reach the end soon. Not that he'll talk to me about it directly. The prince chatters with Father; I can't help but eavesdrop.

Next, Dare tells Ivy how Ilk knows everything that

happens in his mountains. Chances are, the Articae orc will await us at the end of our journey and reopen the mountainside.

If this is Dare's version of courtship, he sucks at it.

- Calla

DAY NINETY-TWO

*D*ear Diary,

We reach the end of the ice road—yay! Now, all that remains is for Ilk to open the mountainside.

Hours pass. Dare is still off doing his own thing. Tristan, Ivy and I fall into an anxious silence. Hanging out in ice caves is a zero on the fun scale. My summer elf side wants to see something green.

Creak.

At last, the cave walls begin to snap and move. Before us, a solid wall of rock breaks apart like curtains on a stage. Outside, there isn't any sign of the Articae Horde, though. Instead, long blue cords weaves through the outer wall, pulling the mountain open.

Ley lines.

My pulse speeds. Those indigo cords can only mean one thing. I rush outside and scan the landscape.

Sure enough, Mother stands on ice beyond. She looks lovely in her flowing gown. In this moment, she truly is the

Blue Fairy, the only elf with the power over the very fabric of time and realms.

And I bet she has no idea that Father's awake.

Tristan marches out from the caves with Dare and Ivy close behind. At last, my parents spot each other. Mother gasps. Father shakes gently.

"You're awake," whispers Mother.

Father sighs. "Blue."

"You're awake!" Mother grabs his skirts and takes off toward Tristan at a run. Father rushes across the ice and snow.

My parents meet in a long hug. Mother leans back. "Where is our Calla?"

The wind bites with cold, and yet I only sense warmth and joy as I step up to my parents and share our very first embrace as family.

Stepping back, Mother checks me over carefully. "You look well. I was so worried."

"It all worked out." Sammy rolls out of my pocket to form a scepter in my hand. "There is a trick to wielding this bad boy, only it's not one you can share."

Mother gives Father a sly look. "You were tempted to just tell her, won't you?"

Father winks. "Of course. Calla figured it out on her own, though."

Mother laughs. In this moment, she's no longer the Ley Queen. Instead, she's my friend Blue. In fact, she's so approachable, I can't help but add in a little commentary.

Growing up, I never had a sibling. Now it feels like I have some healthy competition going on, what with Future Me running around and causing trouble.

"So you know, Father likes *me* the best." I tap my chest for emphasis. "In case you're wondering how I stack up against Future Me."

Mother winks. "Thank you for sharing."

My parents exchange a long smile. These two haven't seen each other in ages. A strange kind of energy fills the air. All of a sudden, I'm wondering how to politely back out of this situation.

It's Father who comes up with a smooth segue. "Will you excuse us for a time?"

"Of course," I say. "Have fun, you two!"

Mother raises her arms. The ley lines that had been weaving through the mountainside now retract into the ground. It raises a lot of questions.

What happens to these ley lines if they die? Do they become ghosts too?

Why didn't Mother do this before? Dare wouldn't have had to call in favors from Ilk.

Wasn't there any way Mother could have been a little more specific about how finding Father would save both him and me?

That said, I already know that it's a waste of breath to ask this stuff. Mother will give me the same answer she always does: *this is the most I can do based on what the ley lines show.*

Speaking of ley lines, they now sprout up from the ground to weave together into a square. Once the grid is in place, it sinks into the ground. Surprise zings through my limbs.

Mother just created a ley pit, right here in the tundra. Who knew that was thing?

My parents lace their fingers together, share yet another sweet smile and then leap right into the pit.

I do a double-take just to be sure the cold isn't freezing my brain somehow. Nope, my parents jumped in and vanished. A moment later, the blue cords dematerialize as well.

Ivy steps up to my side. "This is another queen thing, isn't it? Strange stuff happens to you all the time."

I nod. "It's looking that way, yeah."

The ground rumbles and cracks open as three crystal selkies break through. The first one turns to me.

"Greetings, Queen Calla. Ilk asked us to take you outside of the magical null zone."

This seems to be my hour for double-takes, because I do yet another one. "You can talk?"

"You may call me Prism." He wags his head toward his saddle. "Climb aboard."

I haul myself onto Prism's back. Ivy does the same with her ride.

For his part, Dare steps up to the last crystal selkie in line. "Hello, Moonbeam."

"Your Majesty," says another ice horse who evidently could talk all this time.

I glare at the back of Dare's head. It seems like some people like talking to crystal selkies instead of other people.

So annoying.

- Calla

DAY NINETY-THREE

*D*ear Diary,

Once again, I hold court in the Summer Palace. Blond and Blonder wait by the back doors. Poppa, Muti, Bilge, Oinky and Dare all stand nearby. For his part, Oinky looks especially dapper, considering how he wore a hat for today's court. Tristan and Blue are still off getting reacquainted. I hope they take their time.

The guards look to me. "Ready?" asks Blonder. I've finally figured out how to tell them apart. Blonder parts his hair on the right.

"Let's go!" I call.

The guards pull the doors.

And no one is here.

Yet.

I wave Sammy about. "Let's summon our subjects, buddy."

A flash of golden light radiates out from the scepter to arc into the morning sky. The brightness vanishes into a nearby cloud, which then flares with a golden hue.

I grin. That's my spell finding it's first ~~victim~~ noble.

The cloud pulses with golden light before shooting off another lightning bolt. This one strikes ground on the stretch of palace floor before me. When the brightness vanishes, it leaves behind a new visitor.

Lady Periwinkle. And does she ever look shocked.

I twirl my scepter around, baton style. It's like I'm the leader in my own little parade of awesome. "Hey, Peri."

"My queen," says Lady Periwinkle. "How did this happen?"

"Well, it's like this," I state. "I used my scepter."

"But the Gargoyle King—" begins Peri.

"Got washed away," I interrupt. "Some nasty ice rapids were involved. Looks like all his spells are toast."

"I hope you don't think I was in league with him," says Peri.

"No, I cast a bunch of diving spells. You're good."

Peri points at Ivy. "What is *she* doing here?"

"That's my Butterfly Babe. And I hereby make a new decree. When greeting the Butterfly Babe, everyone must bow low or sing two rounds of *I'm a Little Teapot*." I focus on Peri. "You go first."

Turns out, Peri is a master at the low bow. "Greetings, oh Butterfly Babe."

I tap my chin, debating if I should make her sing anyway. Maybe later. I've got to more nobles to round up.

The process repeats. After waving Sammy, I send more power into the skies. Lightning bolts strike down with new nobles to attend my court.

It's a long day of forcing everyone to show up, greet me and bow to Ivy. Time passes in a snap. Before I know it, court is over and everyone's getting zapped back home. Dare leaves without a major goodbye.

Which doesn't bother me.

Instead, I decide to spend my evening drawing Oinky's portrait. After all, the piggy makes me feel special and wanted.

Unlike *some* people.

- Calla

Oinky

DAY NINETY-FOUR

Dear Diary,

I wake up super early. Actually, it's more like 7 PM. After all my adventures? It certainly feels like crack of dawn. I flutter my eyes open to find Ivy standing beside my bed.

And she's staring at me. So. Creepy.

"I'm here to get you ready," says Ivy.

"For what?"

She doesn't reply. Instead, Ivy makes me bathe in stinky soaps. Then she does my hair and make up. Finally, she helps me slip on a cute pink dress with white trim.

By the time it's all done, I must say I look great.

And Ivy still hasn't told me what she's up to.

"Oh, my," says Ivy at last. "Time to step out onto the balcony."

And do I ever have a sweet balcony off my chambers. There was no way I'd redecorate without one. Ivy pulls open the doors to reveal Dare waiting just beyond the edge.

In a sleigh.

And that thing is being pulled by two winged horses.

He's wearing a dark military jacket, matching pants and an adorable smile. He winks in Ivy's direction. "Thank you, Butterfly Babe."

"Any time!" She waves and skip walks away. That's our Ivy.

I walk out to the balcony's edge. "You brought a sleigh?"

"What?" asks Dare. "You think this mode of transportation is limited to elves with reindeer?"

I grin. The elf that humans call Santa actually lives in Dare's realm. Guess he's kind of a prick. Dare offers me his hand. I step onto his sleigh and we take off.

I've never been in a flying sleigh, so I soak in the view. Before I know it, we've stopped above a crystal blue lake that reflects nearby line of mountains. I'm happy to report that there are no ghosts around.

"What is this place?" I ask.

"Lake Polaris. It's one of my favorite spots in the Winter Realm."

"It's lovely." I soak in the sight of the calm waters, night sky and rolling mountains. "Thank you for bringing me here."

"This is just the beginning. I've some subjects who'd like to meet you."

Down below, the calm surface of the lake breaks. Mermaids rise and wave in my direction. Next a dozen squall birds soar across the skies. They were great white peacocks with wide wings and long tails. Every inch of them seems to glimmer with snow and hope.

On the mountains beyond, pale ice dragons crawl out of their caves and rise on their haunches. Leaning back their necks, they spew great arcs of snow into the air. Their deep roars become a drumbeat that echoes off the mountains.

Down on the lake, lovely elves in white cloaks step out from the depths to stand upon the water's surface. *Sirens.* Using the dragons as their pulsing beat, the sirens sing of the joy that has spread across the winter realm, and all because their prince has found his one true love.

And Dare planned all this for me. Not going to lie. I'm getting a little misty.

The prince looks at me. Pure adoration shines in his dark eyes. "I've been avoiding you lately because once I had your father's blessing, the strictures allow me to kiss you."

Now, I had a big lecture planned about the risks of ignoring people. At this point, I can't remember a word of it. All I can manage is one sound.

"Oh."

"I knew if I got too close to you, I wouldn't be able to control myself. And I wanted our first kiss to be something special." Dare cups my face with his hands, angling our faces until we're only a breath away.

"Am I melting your heart?" asks the prince.

"A little."

Dare places the barest kiss on the shell of my ear.

Along my cheekbone.

Against my eyes.

With every touch of Dare's lips, more heat coils inside me. The prince places a gentle kiss at the very corner of my mouth.

Yes.

Dare grins, and I realize I said that last word out loud.

At last, the prince presses his lips to mine. The touch is the only barest tease of warmth—a whisper of a kiss that sends pure fire heating my veins.

Dare grips my waist, guiding me to sit on his lap. We've done this move before, but in the past I've always had my legs hanging across his. Now we're face to face with my thighs straddling either side of Dare's. All the while, the prince keeps tasting my lips.

More fire builds within me until I can't take it anymore. I slide my tongue along the seam of Dare's mouth. The prince grips my hair, guiding us deeper. I run my hands along his chest, balling my fingers into the fabric of his jacket. Every inch of my body becomes charged with desire.

From the corner of my vision, white lights flicker on my ring hand. More magic.

Dare and I break our kiss. Looking down, I see that my ring has transformed once more. Now the rough string is replaced by thin cords of white silk that twine together into an intricate pattern. I check Dare's hand. The same has happened to him as well.

"What does it mean?" I ask.

The prince presses his forehead against mine. "That we both enjoyed our first kiss."

"Your *very* first?"

Dare nods. "It's always and only been you, Calla."

My heart soars. "Maybe I'll enjoy this courtship ritual."

Dare grins, and a new kind of hunger shines in his eyes. "Oh, I'll make certain of that."

And he does.

The adventure continues with Dare,
Book 3 in the Pixieland Diaries.
Read on for a description!

DARE - BOOK DESCRIPTION

*W*hat happens when a pixie outcast seizes the Faerie throne... but her beloved prince becomes a wanted criminal?

Sassy pixie Calla loves the prankster life. Sure, her trickster ways irritate other fae. In fact, some elves want to exile Calla from Faerie. But then, everything changes. Why? Calla's magic erases an evil blight on the Faerie realm, and so the pariah pixie becomes something unexpected: a Fae Queen.

Yet no sooner does Calla take the crown than a new and unstoppable plague appears. Things get even worse when Calla's longtime crush, the elf Prince 'Dare' Darius, appears to have masterminded the outbreak before fleeing to the mountains. According to the Faerie elders, there's only one way to end this disease...

Calla must hunt down Dare and destroy him.

Yeah. Like that will ever happen.

Instead of killing anyone, Calla vows to cure the plague while proving Dare's innocence. And if she must pull a few mega-pranks to make it all happen? Not a problem. Even so, the path ahead is still fraught with trouble. Secret enemies scheme to manipulate the outbreak—as well as Calla's feelings for Dare—in order to bring our favorite prankster down, once and for all.

Pixieland Diaries Series
1. Pixieland Diaries
2. Calla
3. Dare
4. Lost Prince
5. Ley Queen

FAERIE DRAWINGS

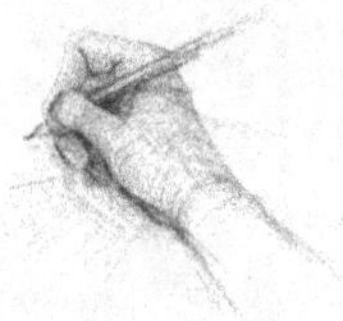

Check out these images from across Faerie! All are drawn by yours truly...

PS. *These pictures are only available in this special enhanced edition because sometimes, we all need extra cool stuff.*

Ley Castle

Butterfly Pixies

Googly Imp

Summer Elf

Pokey the Unicorn

ALSO BY CHRISTINA BAUER

DARE

The adventure continues with DARE, Book 3 in the Pixieland Diaries series!

A modern fairy tale that *USA Today* calls a 'must-read!' Check out WOLVES AND ROSES!

APPENDIX

ACKNOWLEDGMENTS

If you're reading my freaking acknowledgements, chances are, I should thank you for something. So, for the record: you are awesome, dear reader.

That said, huge and heartfelt thanks must go out to my husband and son for their rock-solid support. Writing books means a lot of early mornings, late nights, long weekends, and never-ending patience. You two are the best guys in the universe, period.

After that, I must thank the extensive network of reviewers, friends and colleagues who helped me build my writing chops in general. Gracias.

Finally, deep affection goes out to my late, much loved, and dearly missed Aunt Sandy and Uncle Henry. You saw the writer in me, always. Thank you, first and last.

ABOUT CHRISTINA BAUER

Christina Bauer thinks that fantasy books are like bacon: they just make life better. All of which is why she writes romance novels that feature demons, dragons, wizards, witches, elves, elementals, and a bunch of random stuff that she brainstorms while riding the Boston T. Oh, and she includes lots of humor and kick-ass chicks, too. Christina lives in Newton, MA with her husband, son, and semi-insane golden retriever, Ruby.

Stalk Christina on Social Media

Blog:
http://monsterhousebooks.com/blog/category/christina

Facebook:
https://www.facebook.com/authorBauer/

Instagram:
https://www.instagram.com/christina_cb_bauer/

Twitter:
@CB_Bauer

VLOG:
https://tinyurl.com/Vlogbauer

Web site:
www.bauersbooks.com

AFTERWORD

Dear Reader,

I thought it would be fun to share some important stuff
*—to me, anyway—*about CALLA. Here goes (in no particular
order):

Words, Words, Words

This is probably obvious, but what the heck? The term
faeling is pronounced the same way as the word *failing*… and
faelings are seen as failing both the human and Faerie worlds.
Get it?

Hopefully, at least one person is now surprised.

Poetic Inspiration

The gargoyle summoning spell is inspired by *Tyger Tyger*
by William Blake because WHY NOT? The original version of
this poem also includes the cutest tiger illustration, so I figure
I can offset that sweetness with some bad gargoyle mojo.

The incantation for Dare's courtship ritual is based on To His Coy Mistress by Andrew Marvell. Because that poem is disgusting to women and needed rewriting anyway.

While we're are it, the Gargoyle King's big phrase—*come away with me*—is inspired by a poem from Christopher Marlowe called the *The Passionate Shepherd to His Love*. In this case, I changed things to fit the Gargoyle King's voice more than any personal issues with the poem itself. The original begins with the words "come live with me and be my love."

Sammy The Bouncing Ball

I had real trouble figuring out how Sammy would move and act until I caught my son watching a classic Sesame Street video about Cecile, who happens to be a mega cool bouncing ball. Memba her?

Fairy Tale Inspiration

In every book I write, I try to map the story to a fairy tale. Calla linked with the *Princess And The Frog*. Not because Dare is a frog, but due to the symbolism of the golden ball. In the Grimm's Fairy Tale version, the princess loses her golden ball, an object that some critics take to mean that she's losing her happiness. The journey with the prince is one where the princess must regain her sense of joy about life.

In CALLA, the golden ball also symbolizes personal happiness. In this version, it's the joy of ruling. Learning to wield the scepter is Calla beginning her journey as a joyous queen.

Ben Hur Me, Baby

I love movies, and the 1959 production of *Ben Hur* is one of my favorites. In it, our hero Benny Boy (played by Charlton Heston) wears a ring from a girl as a symbol of his devotion. Then Benny Boy goes off and has tons of adventures but never takes off the ring. He and his girl meet up years later and—*sniff sniff*—he's waited for her all this time. So that inspired me.

I also like the idea of there being a formal courtship process between royals, mostly because that did happen somewhat in medieval times... although mostly through intermediaries. It was nice to imagine a more magical pathway for this to happen.

My Prankster Past

Calla isn't the only prankster I know :) Growing up, my oldest sister was always late getting ready for school. I also had a very hyper dog.

Perhaps you see where this is going.

Instead of waiting patiently inside our family's County Squire station wagon for Miss Thing to get up, I would lock the dog in her room, whereupon it would jump all over her bed until awakening occurred. Yes, it was a prank. But it also taught useful life lessons on what it means to be a working animal (and I include myself in that category).

Backstory

Border Reivers are medieval thieves that raid with abandon. I thought it would be a cool name, and so I built up this whole thing about how Prince Reiver came to Earth in the middle ages and inspired his human counterparts. Then I had to cut that whole backstory out because it didn't move the narrative forward. Maybe it will find another home someday. Most stuff does.

So there you have it—some *random yet critical stuff* about writing this book. I hope you enjoyed it... and that I'll see you again with DARE, Book 3 in the Pixieland Dairies!

Best,

CB

9 781946 677792